Amy
by Any Other Name

Amy by

Any Other Name

Name

Maureen Garvie

KEY PORTER ✒ **BOOKS**

Library and Archives Canada Cataloguing in Publication

Garvie, Maureen
    Amy by any other name / Maureen Garvie.

ISBN 978-1-55470-142-1

I. Title.

PS8563.A6749A79 2009   jC813'.6   C2008-906955-2

ONTARIO ARTS COUNCIL
CONSEIL DES ARTS DE L'ONTARIO

The publisher gratefully acknowledges the support of the Canada Council for the Arts and the Ontario Arts Council for its publishing program. We acknowledge the support of the Government of Ontario through the Ontario Media Development Corporation's Ontario Book Initiative.

We acknowledge the financial support of the Government of Canada through the Book Publishing Industry Development Program (BPIDP) for our publishing activities.

Key Porter Books Limited
Six Adelaide Street East, Tenth Floor
Toronto, Ontario
Canada M5C 1H6

www.keyporter.com

Text design and electronic formatting: Martin Gould

Printed and bound in Canada

09 10 11 12 13 5 4 3 2 1

For Anne Barnett, brave bluff-jumper

Part I

May

SWITCH

So I'm with my grade-eleven class in Toronto on the Thursday before the long weekend. National Skip Day, except Ms. Vesey is making us go on the bus to some dumb-ass play. Can't even remember the name, but it wasn't The Lion King, cause they made us go to that one in grade ten. Bunch of animals running around singing and dancing like a kids' TV show.

I'm heading across the street with Loco and Brittany, and Ms. Vesey's going mad at us like usual when everybody starts going "Krystal! Krystal!" and—pow! I get flattened by a truck. It was turning right on a red, and, I mean, like, we had the green. We had every right to cross.

Next thing I know I'm in the hospital, and I can't move.

Chapter 1

Someone is bending over me, so close I can smell the tuna-salad sandwich she had for lunch. I hate canned tuna. "Krystal?"

She's got the wrong girl. "No, I'm Amy."

The head retracts and whoever it is goes tearing out of the room. I work out right away that I'm in a mess. I can't move my jaw, or much else. I'm like one of those cartoons you see with some guy totally in plaster, hanging by his arms and legs. In my case it's my legs, but my head seems to be in some sort of a wire cage and my arms don't follow orders. So I know that whatever's happened, there goes spring training.

The room fills up. People crowd around the bed. Someone shines a light in my eye. I shut it.

"She's conscious."

"I told you, she tried to speak to me," says the tuna-salad nurse.

A woman in green scrubs asks me, "Can you move your fingers?"

I can't even see my fingers, but I try. I guess I pass the test, because they all cheer.

"Where's my mother?" I mumble. Someone pats my hand.

I repeat the question. What's happened? Mom would be here unless something's happened to her. "Where's Mom?" I howl.

"She's gone home," they tell me. "She was here to see you earlier."

"Am I dying?" I can barely get the words out.

"You've been terribly hurt," they say. "But it'd take more than a truck to kill you."

A truck? What truck? They ask if I'm in pain, and when I say yes, they do something to the bags attached to the tubes that are attached to me. I'm off to la-la land.

I drift in and out of a dream. People I don't know come and sit beside me. They peer into the bird cage that covers my head. They set flowers on the window ledge by my bed and talk at me. Funny old people, some of them, wearing black, with sad faces. Who are they?

I sleep and wake up, sleep and wake up. Still Mom doesn't come. I ask and ask for her, but nobody will tell me why she isn't here.

"You're going for a ride today," the nurse tells me as she adjusts my tubes and wires. "We're moving you to Kingston."

Kingston? But I live in Toronto! I can't say it very well, with my jaw wired up. "Where's my mother?"

"Calm down, calm down," they say. "Take it easy." To make sure I do, they squirt something into my drip.

I sleep through most of the ambulance ride. When I ask why they don't use the siren, they say we're in no hurry. I wake up in Kingston, or that's what they tell me. Everything looks just the same. Mom's not here either.

That night I sense someone moving around the darkened hospital room. A flashlight flickers in my face.

A nurse. "Where's my mother?" I ask.

"Ssshhh."

"Why won't anyone tell me? I have to know." I keep at her, and after a while she goes away and comes back with an answer.

"Your file says she's in Windsor."

"Windsor!" What's she doing in Windsor? We live in Toronto. I try to make that clear. I should know better. Out comes the needle and I'm away to cloud nine again. Mother? What mother?

A physiotherapist comes and moves parts of me around. It hurts and I resist, but after she goes, I think I should have been more co-operative. I have to get out of here. I try to remember what she did and repeat it on my own, but my arms don't even feel like they're mine. There's casts on both of them. I can lift them a little but it hurts so much.

It takes me days to even get one arm up high enough to see my fingers. There's only an inch or so stuck out of the plaster. I wiggle them.

They're white and thick and swollen, and there's dried blood on the cast. Disgusting. They don't look like my fingers—"pianist's fingers," my gran always said, though even that didn't make me practise.

I catch sight of the cuticles—bitten, nasty looking. How did that happen?

But the thing that really weirds me out is the glimpse I get of nail polish. Horrible purplish-black and chipped. Fingernails of the damned.

I struggle to lift my arm again. Did I really see that? I did. I stare and stare. I don't wear nail polish—I'm a jock, a rower. Is this someone's idea of a joke?

I can't lift my arms to touch my face. My tongue knows my teeth are chipped and my lips are cracked and swollen. In the middle of the night a nurse comes in to check out my dials with a flashlight. This time it's a guy. I catch the glint of an earring, gleam of a shaved head. He flicks the beam across my face and sees my eyes are open.

"You're awake." Brilliant. "Naughty, naughty. You need your beauty sleep."

I'd sleep if I could. "I hurt."

"I'll get you something for that." He goes away and comes back with a pill and water. He slips the pill into my mouth, puts the straw between my lips. I suck and swallow.

He tells me his name is Lawrence. "Anything else I can get for you, Krystal?"

"My name's Amy." What's with all this Krystal stuff? Who do they think I am?

"Mirror," I say. That's what I need.

At last he figures out what I'm asking for. "Uh, uh." He shakes his head. "No mirrors. Not a good idea right now, sweetheart. Give it a week. You're not looking your best yet."

I grind my teeth in frustration. When I try the other nurses, they don't even understand me. So the next time it's Lawrence's shift, I ask him again. I bug him until he gives in.

"You're going to freak yourself out, though," he warns. He's gone for an hour and I think he's not going to come back, but then he shows up with a mirror the size of a toonie. He holds it so I can look in it.

I scream.

"Cut out that noise." He whips the mirror back into his pocket and wags a finger in my face. "Shhh! Come on, come on, cut that out. People are trying to sleep."

I stop screaming, and then I remember what I saw and I start again.

"You want to get me in trouble?" He straightens the sheet and tugs my pillow around. "I warned you, but you wouldn't listen. Wait till after those stitches come out. Then you'll be gorgeous again." He scuttles off and comes back with a needle. Pretty soon I can breathe again, but I'm dizzy.

What I saw was my head in a cage, my jaw wired and bolted.

Tracks of stitching across my forehead like Frankenstein's monster. But it's not the stitches, or the bruising like a fading sunset.

It's that no accident I've ever heard of can turn blue eyes brown. I'm screaming because the face I saw in the mirror wasn't mine.

Chapter 2

Morning. The horizon outside the window is a glowing band. Far below is a river, much wider than the one where I used to row on mornings as beautiful as this. This river has green islands in it. I fumble with the button that lowers the bed. I don't like heights anymore.

A nurse comes in to switch bags on the pole by my bed. "What day's it?" I ask her through my head fog.

"Tuesday. Feeling better? No more screaming, I hope. You'll get Lawrence in more trouble than he's usually in."

"How long?" I manage to get out.

She doesn't understand. "They'll be unwiring your jaw in a day or two. That should help with the Frankenstein look."

She means Frankenstein's monster. Frankenstein was the doctor. Everybody gets it wrong. I know, because we took it in school. But I'm in no position to point that out. I shake my head. "How long?" I repeat, and try to say "accident."

Eventually she gets it. "I'm not sure. Three weeks, maybe? You were in intensive care in Toronto before they brought you here."

"Date?"

"You mean, today's?" She checks her watch. "June 25."

But last I remember, it was Victoria Day weekend. That's more than a month ago! "What happened?"

"Honey, you tangled with a truck and the truck won." She says this like it's something witty and takes off before I can ask anything else. Where would I begin?

A truck—the last thing you expect to hit you, diving into a quarry! And how can any accident change blue eyes to brown?

I need to think, and whatever they're putting into my veins makes it hard to do that. When my brain clears a bit, I try.

Clue 1: They think my name is Krystal.

Clue 2: Those fingernails from hell.

Clue 3: Those strange dark eyes under black caterpillar eyebrows.

Clue 4: The truck.

Conclusion: Something has gone terribly, terribly wrong.

I'm beginning to get it. I'm in the wrong body. How wrong can you get? How could it even happen?

Short answer: It couldn't.

On Friday morning, before the start of the long May weekend, I was up by five as usual. Back from rowing in time to get to first-period class, which was English. Then politics with Mr. Ramondo, who was diabolical enough to schedule a test on National Skip Day. "And it will count," he said. But I still managed to bail by eleven, and by noon Gabby, Elly, Damian, Ted, Nate next to me in the front seat, and my dog Wolfie underfoot were breezing up the 400 in the Jeep to my family's island cottage.

We just made it out ahead of the traffic. Mom was coming later. By the time she got off work, it would be crazy on the roads—no point in her leaving the city until after ten. I practically had to sign an affidavit that we wouldn't set the cottage on fire or empty the drinks cabinet or mix up her spice rack, among a long list of other possible sins.

"And drive carefully, Amy," she had to say.

"Mom, I'm responsible."

"Amy, you're sixteen."

I'm a good driver. I've been driving on back roads with Dad since I was twelve. We made it to the lake with no problem, and took the launch to the island. It was hot as July in the cottage when we got there. Unfortunately, the lake was still frigid.

"We can go back to the marina and swim at the quarry," I told everybody. It's only a couple of miles up the road from the town, and the water there warms up much faster than in the big lake. Also, the quarry is one of my favourite places. It's spring-fed, Dad says, so it's clean and clear but not as deep as the lake.

The air smelled like lilacs and phlox. The place I usually jump from is ten feet above the water, but Damian wanted to go higher.

"We need to watch out for the rocks," I warned. I wasn't sure where they were, and with the sun glinting on the water, I couldn't see them.

Gabby made a fuss about all the tadpoles, but the rest of us went in off the top. I remember seeing a hawk circling high above us, hang-gliding on the thermals. Everybody else jumped. I was the only one who dived. I'd done it hundreds of times before, only from a different spot and a lower height. This time I connected with a rock just below the surface.

Fade to black.

A nurse I haven't seen before comes in. I try to tell her what's happened to me. She goes away and that's the last I see of her.

My jaw is unwired, and adjustments are made to my drywall suit. My timelines get confused. I doze uneasily through the days. In the night I leave the broken body in the bed and head out on the river. My arms and legs are light and strong again. I flex my shoulders and skim over the dark surface like a water-strider. There is no ache in my back, no searing pain in my lungs, no rods through my legs. I thrust my feet against the blocks and feel the boat surge.

Still no sign of Mom. The strange old people come and go. I don't speak to them. Maybe they're not real—and if they are, I don't want to encourage them. I'm having one of my rare alert times on an afternoon when two girls sidle in the door with a cone of supermarket flowers. They're wearing little matching plaid skirts with the hems about two feet above their knees, like exotic dancers. They don't give much eye contact, but they take a really good long look at the bolts sticking out of my legs and the pulleys holding me to the ceiling. One's blond. The other's blond with a couple of inches of dark roots.

Dark Roots shoves the cone of flowers at me—blue, artificially coloured carnations. I can't reach it with my arms in plaster, so I mutter, "Thanks."

"It's from our class," says Real Blond. "We all signed the card." So I figure out that the nymphet-hooker outfits are school uniforms. But whose class? Whose school? Not mine, that's for sure.

"Doesn't that hurt?" one asks, pointing at my legs.

"Well, duh," I mumble, and they laugh. It doesn't really hurt, though. I can't feel much of anything. All the drip lines plugged into me are taking care of that.

"You should have seen all the blood," says Dark Roots. "It was so gross. You would have loved it, Krystal."

"Your skirt was right up over your head," says Real Blond. "Good thing you were wearing clean underwear, eh, Brittany?" She giggles.

"I'm not Krystal," I snarl.

"Yeah, right," Brittany snickers. "I forgot, you're the Queen of the Damned."

They natter on, mostly to each other because I don't say

anything back. I'm thinking of screaming: *Fire! Earthquake! Get out of here!* Then a boy carrying a skateboard comes in and they talk to him, and finally, when a nurse tells them only two visitors at a time, they all go. I think I might have dreamed them, but the horrible flowers are on the windowsill for days before the blue goes brown and someone throws them out.

A couple of days later the boy comes back on his own. He's short and stocky with a lot of dark hair and a dirty moustache, like he's been drinking licorice milkshakes. His white shirt hangs over grass-stained pants, a black Ramones t-shirt showing underneath, and a dark green tie overtop. More school uniform, I guess. "Hey," he says. He looks at me—my eyes—sideways, but at least he's making an effort. "I heard you got amnesia."

I grunt.

"You know who I am?"

"No."

"Cool. You know who you are?"

"Amy Wexford. I'm not Krystal."

He grins and starts talking about some movie he's seen in which the main character gets amnesia and has to kill to get his memory back. I shut my eyes and think homicidal thoughts. At least his voice isn't like fingernails against a blackboard, like Real Blond and Dark Roots. I drift off, and when I wake up, he's gone.

I concentrate hard on remembering. More is beginning to come back. Driving to the quarry with the gang and Wolfie in the Jeep. I was hyperconscious of Nate's shoulder brushing mine. When I asked him a week before in the cafeteria if he wanted to come with us for the weekend, he looked surprised. I was surprised I'd dared. I didn't know him that well, just wanted to. He only moved to our school from St. Andrews after Christmas, and kind of kept to himself. I figured he was shy, but he was good-looking in a skinny, broad-shouldered, dark-eyed kind of way. A head of curly black hair, a jaw like some cowboy hero, and sort of a long nose. Not that tall, but an inch or two on me—five foot eleven, maybe.

So when I dived from the top, maybe I was showing off a bit for him.

A bit? A lot.

After that, I remember almost nothing. Only the yellow light—brilliantly, gloriously bright, drawing me to it. But it was so far off, down a very long, dark corridor, and I was running to it as fast as I could. I ran past shadowy figures, hundreds of them, crouched or leaning against the walls in the gloom. They were waiting, they'd been waiting for ages, for who knows how long. But I wasn't waiting, I was priority-rated. I was going right to the head of the line. I was speeding towards the sun to freedom.

But no—I'm going too fast. Back up.

There was something before that, I remember. People around me, bending over me, shouting like in an *ER* rerun when something goes wrong, machines sucking and beeping and blaring. But I'm not there on the gurney. I'm up above somehow, looking down on my long, sheet-covered body. Getting ready to leave it. So sad, too bad, but goodbye, goodbye. Then I'm on my way, eagerly hurrying toward the light.

Oh, I'm going, I'm nearly there. I'm stretching out my stride—it's like being out on the water in the boat, feeling my muscles kick in. But something pulls me back again, against my will. I don't like it. I see my mother, not in the room with me and all the doctors but somewhere close. Her face is in her hands, her lovely hair messy and flopping. "Amy, Amy, oh Amy," she moans. "Hang on, darling, please, please hang on."

My father sits beside her, his arm awkwardly around her shoulder. But it's too late, they're split, divorced, there's all that anger between them.

jfaced, sick with fear—poor Nate, what'd he get himself in to? And

I want to tell them, "Don't worry, I'm okay, everything's great," but I have to go, I really do, I can't wait any longer. Besides, this is going to be fantastic!

I'm picking up the pace, faster and faster, and I'm almost at the end of the tunnel. I'm so happy now, throwing in a little skip and a hop, singing. It's going to be like heaven and Muskoka and Gran's house all in one.

Suddenly a figure looms in my path. I swerve to avoid it, but we collide. I swear and lurch to one side and fall. I'm screaming now, lashing out in fury. *Goddammit you clumsy, stupid jerk! You idiot! Get out of my way! I was almost there! I was almost to the light!*

Hands pull at me roughly. Machines suck my soul. I don't want to come back, it's agony for me. I fight to get free, but I'm roped in and stuffed back inside. I'm suffocating. This body is too tight, it's like an old pair of outgrown shoes. My loosed spirit has already begun to expand and grow. I'm way too big now for that miserable, broken piece of flesh.

I lose the fight. They win.

"That was close," I hear someone above me say.

"Bad start to the night. And the long weekend's only just started."

"Mostly kids too. It's always the same. The one in OR2 didn't look like she was gonna make it."

Chapter 3

In the hospital in Kingston I wake up at night again. It isn't the pain that wakes me. I don't feel a thing, even with my legs cranked in the air, dangling from a metal bar. From the neck down my body's a blur.

I wiggle my fingers, anxious. They report in okay. But then I already knew I could move them. I try to wiggle my toes, and I think I can move them too, but I'm not sure. It could be only imagination. I've heard that even after people have their legs cut off, they still can feel itches or pains in their feet and legs. Phantom limbs, they call them.

The mounds in the other beds in the room breathe and snuffle. Voices murmur up and down the corridor, and footsteps pad past the open door. I grope for the button that makes the head of my bed go up, and raise myself so that I can look out over the river and the dark islands. A few lights twinkle on the far shore. I lie watching wispy clouds move across the night sky, thinking of Mom sobbing my name in the hospital hallway, Dad with his arm around her. Where is she now? Probably in bed at home, knocked herself out with her famous "half-a-tranq." Maybe my sister has come to stay with her for a while, or one of my aunts might be there.

Does Mom think I'm dead? Poor Mom. I have to let her know I've hung on.

But what happened to my body, my real body, my Amy body? Did it die?

And then I think: *If I'm in the body of some little black-finger-nailed loser, does that means she's in mine?*

Retroboy is hunched in the chair by my bed again, pushing his skateboard back and forth with his feet. I see him check out the hair growth on his upper lip with his tongue when he thinks I'm not looking.

He catches my eye. "You really got amnesia? You don't know who I am? You don't know my name?"

Not a clue. "Jason?" A stab in the dark. His mother probably named him after some soap star. "Lance?"

He shakes his head.

"Darren?"

He frowns.

"Christian? Thorne? Yogi Bear? Rumpelstiltskin?"

He cracks a smile. "You got close there."

"Rumpelstiltskin?"

"No, I meant Yogi. It's Loco." He beams. "Loco. Crazy man."

"Yeah, right, Loco. Look, I need to call someone. I can't reach the phone." I gesture with my head to the far side of the room to demonstrate the obvious. "Can you bring it over for me?"

"What about them?" He ducks his head at my two room-mates.

They've moved me in with an old lady who groans all the time, and somebody else behind a curtain, so she's in really bad shape. "I don't see either of them needing the phone right now."

He gets up reluctantly and pulls the cord out the wall, plugs it into the jack above my bed, then lifts the receiver. "Got a dial tone." He holds it out, looking pleased with himself.

My palms are sweating. "My mother." But I can't hold the phone with both my hands in casts. "Dial for me, will you?" I tell him the number with the area code. "It's long distance. Dial one first."

He punches it in, his face screwed up in concentration.

I'm having trouble breathing. What am I going to say when she answers? Or worse, if I have to leave a message. *Uh, Mom, I've been kidnapped by somebody else's body. Could you come and get me?*

Sure.

But then I see her sobbing in the hospital corridor, and I know I have to reach her. Does a body really matter? The important thing is that I'm still here, that I'm alive! When I hear her voice, I'll know the right thing to say.

Loco listens, holds the phone to my ear. My blood is pounding so loud I can hardly hear above it. A recorded voice. "*Long distance service is not available to this subscriber. Please hang up.*"

Loco shrugs. "It won't take the call."

"Do you have a cellphone?" I ask frantically.

He shakes his head. What a useless jerk.

The little old people shuffle in the next day, a man and a woman, wrinkly. I remember them dimly. She's tiny, with thick white hair that looks like it might be a wig, but I don't think it is, because I can see her pink scalp.

"How are you now, Krystiana?" the old man asks solemnly. He has a big nose and caterpillar eyebrows and hair sprouting out of giant ears shaped like portobello mushrooms.

How does he think I am? How do I look? I don't know what to say to them, so I shut my eyes and pretend to be asleep. They sit by my bed for a while and mutter to each other in a language I don't understand. Then they get up and go.

A woman I haven't seen at all before drops by a day or two later. "Do you know who I am yet, Krystal?" she asks.

Yet? Has she been here before? I shake my head. I don't know anybody in this life.

She's old, forty maybe, grey-streaked hair pulled back in a ponytail. She's a bit on the heavy side, swaddled in a denim shirt and baggy jeans. If I had to sum her up in a word—well, I don't know what it would be, but it wouldn't be fashionista.

"I'm Joan. Your foster mother. They said you were having problems remembering, that it might take a while before your memory comes back." She gives me a good long look. "You sure you're not faking it, Krystal?"

I frown at her. "Who are you?"

She sighs. "You've been living with me since June last year. I came in to see you a few days ago, but you were out having an X-ray."

"Where's my real mother?"

"In Windsor, far as I know. She says she'll try to come and visit if she can get time off. She said to tell you she'll do her best to come." She pauses and takes a breath. "I don't want you to count on it and be disappointed, though. You know she's promised before and it didn't work out."

I know it isn't my mom we're talking about, but this woman in Windsor, she's a mother! "But I could have died!"

"I know, I know. She said she went to see you in the hospital in Toronto but you weren't conscious."

"And that's it? That's the only chance I get?" I'm getting really mad, and confused, because it's not even my mother, it's this Krystal person's mother. But what kind of mother can't spare the time to visit when her daughter just escaped death by a hair? When her daughter's lying in a hospital bed, maybe paralyzed?

Joan shrugs. "You know your mother. She tries her best."

"That's why you're the foster mother, right?"

She goes on about some other kids of hers, Paige and Jordi and Leanne. "I don't suppose you'll be wanting your school books for a while. I guess this is the best excuse you'll ever have for not doing your homework." She checks her watch. "I should go get the girls from school. Is there anything else you need from your things?"

"I can't think of anything I want," I say. I can't imagine what this Krystal would have that I would ever want—not her fingernails or her face or her friends or her skanky mother.

"You'll be needing your clothes eventually. I'll try to come in again before that, but you know how things can be at home. I hear Raymond is coming to see you. You can always send me a message through him, if you think of something." She gives the cast on my arm nearest to her a pat and goes.

Raymond?

Turns out that's Yogi, Loco, whatever. Today he's wearing a Dandy Warhols T-shirt under the same dirty white shirt unbuttoned and hanging over his pants. "What *is* your name?" I ask him. "Don't tell me it's Raymond."

He winces, then scowls. "Raymond's a shit name. It's Loco. Everybody calls me Loco."

"Oh, yeah? And is that good or bad?"

Now he grins. "Bad. I'm bad, man."

Not that bad. I've seen *real* bad in Toronto, let me tell you. In-your-face, drive-by, don't-mess-with-me bad, and this one's nowhere near it. He's not even junior bad. The real ones would chew this puppy up and spit him out without breaking stride. "I don't like Loco," I say. "I don't think it's good to be labelled crazy. I'm calling you Loki." No special reason, it just pops into my head.

He starts to protest.

"It's a great name. It's some kind of Norse god," I tell him. "The trickster, I think."

He's still frowning, like he's not sure. I don't want to argue with him. Really, I don't care, but I don't want to piss him off so much he won't come back. "How tall am I?" I ask.

"Huh? Not very."

"Can you be more exact?"

He shrugs again. "Five foot, uh, two?"

Gasp. "And I was worried all those years about being too tall."

"Geez, your brain's scrambled." He grins happily.

"So tell me again how it happened. Tell me about the truck."

He folds his arms. "Well, we were, like, in Toronto, eh, just crossing the street, following everybody else, you know, horsing around and stuff. And then *wham*! This truck comes through the intersection and picks you up and bounces you off the traffic light. Man, it just missed me too."

"It didn't run over me?"

He screws up his face, remembering. "It might have, uh, run over your leg. Legs. When you slid down the traffic light."

"And what did you do? Was I bleeding? Breathing? Did you give me mouth-to-mouth resuscitation?"

His eyes are on mine, but he's looking through me. He blinks, and I can see he's right back there when it happened. He swallows hard. His mouth twists up and he covers his face with his hands.

Oh god. I don't know why I'm needling him, taking it out on him. It's not his fault. But it's too late to take it back, nothing I can do. I stare at the ceiling and wait. When I turn my head back toward him, I catch him wiping his eyes on his sleeve.

"I didn't mean to upset you."

"Who's upset?" he growls.

"It's not your fault if somebody walks into a truck." I almost add, "It's okay, don't worry, I'll be all right." Looking after other people's feelings is an old habit of mine, but it doesn't make much sense now. One day they'll crank this body out of traction, maybe even get it walking again. But who's going to get me back to *me*?

And I think, if he's feeling so bad, he can do something to

help. "There's something you can do for me, Loki. Can you find me a cellphone? *Please?*"

"Where do I get one of those?" He frowns. "You think I got that kind of money?"

"I have no idea. But see what you can do."

Chapter 4

He doesn't come back the next day, or the day after. I begin to worry I pushed him too far and he won't come back. Not that I care about some grubby little skater boi, but he seems very loyal to this Krystal. I guess he must have liked her. And I'm not so out of it I don't know I need all the help I can get.

The service is mostly good and the nurses are mostly nice, but the food is awful. Everything they say about hospital food is true: overcooked carrots and peas, not enough protein to rebuild broken bones. They don't even cook the meals on the premises—the nurses tell me they're trucked in from Ottawa. Ottawa! That's over a hundred miles away. And they don't know the meaning of "organic." At least the nurses will spoon in as much yogourt as I can take.

The worst part is, there's no end in sight. They're forever wheeling me off for X-rays and scans and ultrasounds and MRIs, but when I try to find out what's going on, when I'm going to get this body moving, no one gives me a straight answer. Doctors breeze through on their rounds but it's hardly ever the same one twice. Apparently I'm the patient of some hotshot named Morrison, but the guy could be a myth for all I know. I don't think he's ever seen me out of anaesthetic.

And the horrible, scary part is nobody will tell me if I'll be able to walk again. When I keep bugging them, the therapist finally comes back and gives me more exercises. This time I pay attention. I work on them when there's nothing else to do, which is most of the time. But when I ask her when the monster bolts are coming out of my knees, she plays dumb. "I'll see if I can find out from Dr. Morrison," she says.

Three days later, Loki comes through the door. He's fishing in his pocket and holding something up. A cellphone!

"Took you long enough," I grumble, but I'm so glad to see him my nose starts to run.

He shrugs. "I gotta get it back right away. But you can use it now."

I take a deep breath. "It's a long-distance call. It'll be expensive, okay? But I'll pay."

"How you gonna do that?"

Good point. I stare at the thing, a real old clunker. Loki doesn't even know how to use it—what planet does he live on? I tell him how to turn it on and get him to punch in the numbers.

Take complete breaths—belly, ribs, collarbone. He holds the phone to my ear.

"Hello?"

Mom's voice! The familiar sound flows over me, overwhelms me. "Mom, it's me, it's me, Amy!" I gasp. "It's Amy!"

Silence on the other end.

"Hello?" I'm panicking. "Mom, can you hear me?"

"I can hear you," she says. "Who *is* this?"

I rush on. "Mom, it's me, *me*, Amy. I'm alive, I'm in the hospital in Kingston. Come and get me, please come and get me. You won't recognize me, they think my name is Krystal. There's been some terrible mistake. Come and get me. Oh, Mom, I love you!" I finish on a wail.

Long silence.

"Hello? Mom, say something, please!" The phone has slipped away from my ear. I flop my head at Loki. "Hold it up, hold it up!"

When Mom speaks again, her voice is cold. I've heard her talk to telemarketers in that tone. "I don't know who this is, but if this is your idea of a joke, you must be a sick young woman. My daughter is in the hospital still in very serious condition, as I'm sure you know. If you think it's funny to torment people under these circumstances, you're despicable."

And then silence. There isn't even a click.

"Mom, Mom!" Nothing. The line's dead. "Mom!" I scream.

"Shut up! Shut up!" Loki hisses, sticking his face an inch away from mine and glaring. When I don't shut up, he looks wildly around and grabs a folded blanket. He's advancing, holding it with both hands, like he's going to smother me with it. I shut up.

"I told you you shouldn't call," he growls over my sobbing. "That bitch doesn't care nothing about you." His hands still clench the blanket. "You set yourself up for it. Why'nt you forget her, like she forgot you?"

"What do you mean, calling her a bitch?" I whimper. Why is he making judgments about my mother? He doesn't even know her.

"You called her that too. She goes off to Windsor with that guy and doesn't even tell you she's leaving? She's a bitch all right."

It's Krystal's mother he means. "I'm not Krystal."

He snorts. "You're crazy." He amends it. "You got amnesia."

"Not amnesia." I try to tell him what happened, how Krystal and I started to die at the same time and bumped into each other on the way to the light and never made it. And how we got back in the wrong bodies. After a while he lays down the blanket. And starts telling me the plot of *Freaky Friday*.

Before he goes he hunts around on the bed for the phone. He

sees me staring at it miserably.

"It's Brittany's sister's." He stuffs it in his pocket. "She'll kill me and Brittany both if I don't get it back. It's not gonna do you any good anyway. And I'm not bringin' it again."

The night is a bad one—no surprise. Most nights are bad. I'll get an itch under my arm or on my butt and it'll drive me nuts not being able to scratch it. Tonight what keeps me awake is Mom's voice in my head.

"*Who is this?*" she asks.

"*Who is this?*"

She sounds so harsh, so angry, so mean. I play it over and over, trying to try to change it, but I can't, and I lie there crying for a long time. I'm sticky and sweaty and smelly, just about crazy. I'd give anything to get up, pad into my bathroom, and take a lovely cool shower. The thought gets me crying even louder. I feel so utterly alone.

Why don't I yell, scream and not stop until I make them understand? Why don't I prove the truth with facts, numbers, my grandmothers' maiden names? But I've tried, I've tried over and over, and all they do is fill my veins with drugs and shut me down.

"*Who is this?*" My own mother doesn't recognize me. It's a stranger's voice she hears. Well, it's not my voice, is it? It's Krystal's voice I'm stuck with. "My daughter is in the hospital," she said. Her *daughter*—I'm her daughter. So who's that in the hospital?

I know who it is.

Lawrence is working the night shift again, and he comes in and sees I'm awake. Right away he's on my case. "Hear you've been stirring up trouble again." There's a spy in the room now, another patient, some busybody of an old slag named Della who thinks I want to hear all about her grandchildren.

"You tell your boyfriend to keep his cellphone out of here

unless he wants to get banned," Lawrence warns me.

"He's not my boyfriend."

"Tell *him* that. But you'll get better and out of here a lot faster if you improve your attitude." Then he softens. "I know it's tough, poor kid. Want me to get something to help you sleep?"

I shake my head at first, but then I weaken, and swallow the pill, along with the water in the cup he holds to my lips.

"You need sleep," he says. "You need it to heal."

But I can't get used to sleeping in public, nurses checking for vital signs at four a.m. and strangers snoring in the next beds. At home I never had to sleep in the same room with anyone. My sister Meaghan is a lot older than me, eleven years. I was thirteen when she got her own condo. I moved too, out of my pink princess room to the loft on the third floor. Mom says it's grim, and Meaghan says I must be obsessive-compulsive. She should talk. But I like things minimal and tidy.

I like things neat. I've always been that way. I can't think properly in a mess. When I lie in bed, I don't want to see anything but bare walls and treetops out the window and the sky through the skylights, birds swooping past in the morning and evening, and at night, the stars. My loft room is my haven. Sometimes I have friends stay for sleepovers, but I actually prefer to be on my own. Wolfie is enough company for me. I wonder if he's missing me, poor darling. Sometimes in here I forget where I am and I dream that the weight of my cast is his big furry body against my legs.

Lawrence comes by one more time, and at last I drift off to sleep. I dream I'm rowing again, this time with the team. I can't see the others—I think Gabby and Jenn are there. Whoever they are, I know them as well as I know myself. They breathe as I breathe. Our blood pumps as if powered by a single heart. We bear down in perfect rhythm as the oars catch. The keel barely touches the surface, the water's a mere whisper against the boat's skin. We're flying, and I'm feeling no pain.

Brittany of the dark roots and plaid tutu slouches in the next day with her sidekick of the blond roots, now with pink streaks. They talk about teachers and new songs, hot boys they're going to do and other slutty girls that better stay out of their way.

I nod and nod and say, "Uh-huh," and that seems to be enough for them. I'm listening to them, aren't I? Probably nobody else does.

They cut classes all the time and they don't seem to do any sports or go anywhere except some place called Jimmy's to hang and play pool. On second thought, I guess pool is a sport. But don't they care about marks? They don't seem to have any concept that they're going to need them if they want any kind of life.

Loki comes in and they have to leave, because of the two-visitors rule. Loki's here a lot lately, almost every day.

"Is the hospital on your way home from school?" I ask him.

He rolls his eyes like I've said something stupid again. "I get a bus."

"Your boyfriend's very loyal," the nurses tease me.

"He's not my boyfriend." For one thing, he'd come up to my ear if I was in my right body. For another, I don't think he's that bright. I wonder if there's much in his head except skateboarding and computer games and bad videos. Let him get started on this movie his mom/brother/loser friends rented the night before, and he'll tell you the whole thing right to the end. Once he gets going, it'd take a truck to stop him—speaking as one who supposedly knows.

Some days, though, I admit it's kind of soothing, letting him garble on about *Vampires of Suburbia* or some pointless alien attack. Or some chick-flick of his mom's that he seems to think I'd like. It makes me think about being cuddled up with my own mom on the couch with a giant bowl of popcorn, watching one of her corny old movies. *The Thin Man*, maybe, or *Gone with the Wind*.

No matter what the plots are, Loki's happy when he's telling me about them. I don't think anyone listens much to him either.

The spooky old people show up again, the tiny old woman and the man with the grass growing in his ears. I don't have the excuse of the wired jaw anymore, so I play possum. "Krystiana," pleads the old woman, trying to hold my fingers, "don't you know your *ava* and *avo*?"

At least that's what I think she says. They talk to each other in their strange language, and the old woman starts to cry. The old man takes her hand, and they shuffle away. I breathe a sigh of relief.

"I know you're awake there, girl," snaps Della from the next bed. "It wouldn't have killed you to have said hello to your poor old grandparents. Christ, I'm dying for a cigarette."

Grandparents? "They're no grandparents of mine." But I'm feeling kind of bad, making that old woman cry. I know it wouldn't have killed me to say something to her. But I'm sorry, my life's complicated enough already.

Chapter 5

Next morning the mythical Dr. Morrison makes a special guest appearance. I'm honoured. He's perfectly cast for a surgeon, short grey hair and steel-rimmed glasses, the right mix of caring and wise. He pulls the curtain around us and cozies up to the bed. "I'll bet you're getting a little tired of being strung up here like a chicken," he says.

"Chicken?" I'm tired of being strung up for sure, but I don't get his metaphor. "Who'd put a chicken in traction?"

He gives a short bark of laughter. "The last set of X-rays show you're coming along very well, Krystal. We'll be taking the hardware out of your legs and giving you a new cast, so that you can start moving around a bit more."

My heart leaps. "When?"

"Soon as we can schedule it. What else would you like to know?"

"Will it hurt?"

"You won't feel a thing. We'll do it under general anaesthetic."

"And then will I be able to walk?"

I don't get a third question. He gives me another dose of that bedside smile, yanks open the curtain, and breezes away to some golf course.

"I guess you'll be glad to get out of that," Della pipes up.

I will. I've been very jealous of Della, hopping into her wheelchair and taking her drip on its pole down in the elevator whenever she wants a smoke. "What did he mean about a strung-up chicken?"

She rolls her eyes and clicks the remote at her TV. "You want me to turn up the sound so you can hear? Do you good to think about something besides yourself. It's one of them extreme makeover things."

Five minutes later, she clicks it off again. "I can't believe anybody would be stupid enough to put themselves through that if they didn't have to," she snorts. "'Trussed up,'" she adds. "He meant trussed up like a chicken. Stuffed and sewed up, like for Sunday dinner."

"That's not a very sensitive thing for him to say to somebody in my shape."

"He's a surgeon. Comes with the territory."

None of the nurses can tell me when my de-trussing is supposed to happen. So when a new person carrying a file folder sticks her head around the door and asks for Krystal, I hope she's come to tell me my operation's been scheduled.

She has a nice face. At first I think she's maybe thirty or so, but close up she has wrinkles. She's probably even older than my mother. "Hello, Krystal," she says, smiling. "I'm Susan McGuire, from the Family Medicine unit."

"Do you know when they're taking me out of traction?"

"I'm afraid not. Actually, I'm not a doctor. I'm a psychologist."

Oh, wonderful. "They told you I was crazy?"

"Not at all." She gestures at my feet in their rig and my heavy-duty full body cast. "All this is a serious trauma for you to process. If we talk it through, it may make it easier for you to get back to normal."

Back to normal! Right. "My name's not Krystal. It's—" I'm about to say "Amy," but something in my head makes a last-minute adjustment. Because I'm not Amy anymore, Amy with the nice house and loft bedroom and her own cell and high-speed Internet. I'm sure not Krystal either. "Mia," I say. "It's Mia."

"Well, Mia," says Susan, not missing a beat, "tell me about what's happened to you."

So I tell her. She asked, didn't she?

I start right back at the quarry. I've told the story to myself over and over, but it's another thing to be telling it to a stranger. All the time I'm talking, Susan's face doesn't give anything away. When I finish, she sits there for about a minute and doesn't say a word.

I can wait.

Just when I'm about to scream she opens her mouth. "And how do you think that could happen?"

Good question.

I give her my theory from what I've been told and what I remember. How I must have gone into cardiac arrest on the operating table. I tell her about going to the bright light, and Mom and Dad calling me back. "And I did come back, but to the wrong body. And I think that happened to this Krystal girl too, and we somehow made a mistake getting back into our bodies. We got into the wrong ones."

"You think—Krystal—is in yours?"

"Yeah, I guess so. Anyway, I'm in hers."

I can't read her expression. "Do you believe me?" I prompt her, my heart racing. Now I can see her thinking: *Mustn't upset this wacko.*

"I don't think you're lying," she says finally.

"Just crazy, right?"

"What you've told me doesn't make any sense according to what I know about how the world works," she says slowly. "But you're very lucid and convincing."

"Thanks."

We sit in silence for a while. When her pager goes off in her purse, I think I see relief flicker across her face. She concentrates on checking the message.

Then she looks back at me. "I'll have to go now, I'm afraid. Can you give me a little time to think about what you've told me?"

"Sure. You'll come back?"

"As soon as I can." She checks her agenda. "Thursday?"

And this is Monday. I shut my eyes. "Okay."

The days until Thursday are agony. I wake up in the night sweating. I'm sure I've made an awful mistake opening my mouth again. They'll ship me off to the psych ward. I saw *Girl, Interrupted*. I know you don't get out of those places for years, if ever. I shouldn't have trusted that Susan woman. She just reminded me of somebody my mother might know. I thought she had a kind face.

All of a sudden my secret feels so terribly dangerous, something they could put me away for. Why haven't I ever heard of what happened to me happening to another human being? It must have—how could I be the first? Maybe because if anybody tried to talk about it, they threw them straight into the loony bin and threw away the key.

I get paranoid, thinking the nurses are talking about me in the hall. I see Della giving me fishy looks. I thought she was watching television when Susan came, but she must have been eavesdropping with half an ear.

Am I crazy? Am I really Krystal after all? Krystal goes to a school where the girls dress like waitresses in a tartan bar. She has a skater-boi boyfriend with his ass hanging out of his pants. I close my eyes and search the blackness in my brain for any scrap or trace of being Krystal. I try to remember going to that school of hers. I try to remember living in a foster home with Joan and all those the kids. Nothing comes.

Krystal's mother—nothing. Krystal's mother dumped her and went off to live with some guy. My mother would never, ever do that.

She wouldn't leave me. She's never been one of those helicopter moms hovering around making sure everything's okay, but she loves me. She's got a career—she doesn't have time to stay home and bake cookies all day, but who does? If anything ever really went wrong, she'd be there.

Until now.

Krystal doesn't have a father. I do! Allan Ronald Wexford, forty-nine years old, call me Al. So he doesn't live with us anymore, but that's the same with half the kids I know. Dad and I talk on the phone a couple of times a week. He still calls me by my old baby nickname, "Bunny." I'm welcome at his condo anytime. Just call ahead, make sure he doesn't have a heavy date.

I've got a sister, Meaghan. She's tall and smart and she used to spend lots of money on corporate clothes. Now she has a baby girl and spends lots of money on childcare and educational toys.

I've got a dog. My poor darling Wolfie. Wolfie's nothing like a wolf, by the way. He got called that as a joke, when he was a puppy, about as predatory as a banana muffin. I mean, he's a golden retriever.

I can't imagine a single place in Krystal's life. I can't see her room, I can't see a bed with her old teddy on the pillow. But I can walk through every room in my house, from the front hall with its antique bench and coat rack to the kitchen all the way up to my room on the third floor. I can look out the skylight into the branches of the big maple tree. A couple of years ago a snarl of tape from an old cassette caught in it like Christmas tinsel. In summer the leaves hide it, but in the autumn when the leaves fall, I can still see it. No matter how hard I try to think of being in Krystal's space, in Krystal's head, in Krystal's skin, I can't see anything at all.

Chapter 6

Thursday morning arrives. **Then** it's noon, another horrible lunch, and no Susan. She never told me what time to expect her. When I finally see her in the doorway at three o'clock, I feel a huge rush of relief. Even better, I don't see any guys in white suits ready to haul me off to the nut house.

"I didn't think you were coming back."

"What made you think that? I promised you I would." She has these glasses on an old-lady string around her neck. She puts them on for a minute to look at me and smiles, then pushes them up on top of her head like sunglasses.

"I thought after what I told you, you wouldn't want to. You'd be too weirded out."

"People have told me all kinds of things, Krystal."

"It's Mia, remember?"

"I'm sorry. Mia. I won't forget again. Can we talk some more, about your Toronto life?"

So I tell her, about my parents and my sister and my dog. I tell her about my parents splitting. I tell her my mom started selling real estate, how she's very good at it. I come from a family of high-achieving women. My sister is even more into competing than me. She has this big high-stress job in the Ministry of Health. When she had the baby, she practically just took the afternoon off to go to the hospital and then went back to work.

"Keep going," Susan says.

I tell her about our house, my school, my teachers. I talk about how I row on the school team and how we won the championship last year. I tell her about my best friends Gabriella and Elly, Damian, and Ted. And Nate, but I don't say much about him, because what is there to say? It was mostly a feeling I had about him and I think he had about me. We didn't have time for anything more.

"You could have read all that in a book," Susan says gently. She asks me some skill-testing Toronto questions. "What's the closest subway stop to your house?"

"Davisville."

"How do you get to school?"

"Avenue Road bus up to Lawrence."

She asks how I'd get to the Science Centre, where I shop for clothes. I tell her about my favourite places, one on Eglinton and one on Queen. I tell her about Latifa's, the place we all go for coffee.

She asks where my parents were born, where my grandparents came from. I'm a bit foggy about the ancestor stuff. I have to admit I was never all that interested. "I don't know." I panic. "Now you won't believe me!"

She pats my arm in its cast, frowning. "It's not a question of believing you, Mia. I grew up in Toronto, the Bayview area, and everything you've told me fits. There could be some way you're making all this up, some way you've found out all this information, but I don't know how . . . or why you'd want to."

She's looking me in the eye. "I've been in this business for quite a while. What you've told me about going to the light—I've heard a couple of people describe that experience, people who nearly died. I suppose you might have read about it somewhere."

"Is that what you think?"

"I'm not saying that." Then she says, "When I was a little older than you, I spent a couple of years in India. I was twenty-two. That probably seems old to you, but now it seems to me I was terribly young. I never got over it. That experience taught me so many things, one of them being that the human spirit has dimensions our culture knows little about. We have a very narrow, fearful view of what the universe holds. What you've just told me doesn't fit that view."

"I know. But do you believe me?" I desperately want her to say yes.

"I said before I didn't think you're lying. I'm sure you're not."

That's as far as she'll go, but it's enough. I start snuffling.

When she goes, she promises she'll come back soon. I lie there for a long time thinking. Next time she comes, I'll find some way to prove it to her beyond a doubt. I'll tell here something that I'm the only one in the world who could know, something she could check without anyone thinking she was snooping. The address of my gran's house in Leaside. The name of my rowing coach at the club. Dad's latest girlfriend.

At first I get excited thinking of other things I can say to convince her. But even if she believes me, what difference is that going to make? How is that going to get me out of this body and back to me?

And then I think, what if my body, my real Amy body, with Krystal in it, dies? What if she's already died! That freaks me out so much I start to shake. I remember the words my mother said in that terrible phone call: "*My daughter is in the hospital still in very serious condition.*"

"Still," she said, though. "Still" is different from just "in very serious condition." Makes it sound like that's not the way it's always going to be. Like her daughter's going to live.

Friday morning—surprise!—someone comes to wheel me off to the OR. I wake up afterwards feeling groggy but wearing a lot less plaster. There's a boot on one foot, a cast on one thigh, a couple of plaster gauntlets on my wrists. I'm still in a body cast, but they tell me I'll have a plastic one soon. Best of all, the bolts through my legs are gone.

My stubby little hands look cleaner. The last of the nail polish is gone—they must have really scrubbed me down. It's horribly embarrassing, thinking about being naked with Krystal's breasts, in front of who knows how many people. I used to be a 36A and I have an idea that Krystal is a lot bigger in that regard. I wasn't conscious, and it wasn't my body anyway, but that they thought it was my body makes it worse somehow.

"As soon as those holes in your leg heal, we'll be shipping you off to St. Mary's for rehab," the nurse tells me as she tucks me back into bed.

"Will I be able to walk?"

"That's what rehab is for."

Not a straight answer, but I'll be glad to get out of here.

They've already phoned Joan, Krystal's foster mom, to bring me some clothes. She comes in with a big plastic supermarket bag of things I wouldn't be seen dead in, ha, ha: a black denim mini with a pleated frill at the bottom, and ghastly black platform boots made out of some kind of shiny plastic.

"I can't wear those!"

She looks pained. "You won't be wearing any of them for a while. But you don't own anything better."

I can imagine. "Does she have anything that isn't black?"

She gives me another look. "Everything *you* have is black. The past six months, it's all you'd wear. Now you've changed your mind?"

"There isn't anything, like, brown? Or maybe grey or navy blue?"

She sighs. "I'll have a look at Goodwill."

"Watch for Tommy Hilfiger labels," I mutter.

Della calls over, "She's been going on to them again about that 'wrong body' stuff."

Joan closes her eyes for a moment, then turns to talk to Della. "She's not a bad kid," she says. "She doesn't like anybody to know it, but it's true. She's real good with the little ones at home—yes, you are, Krystal, even though you complain."

Della goes all holy. "It's a terrible thing that's happened to her, the accident, but she could look at it as a chance to change her life. To turn it around. God works in wondrous ways."

"That he does," Joan agrees.

"I'm still here," I remind them. "You can speak to me directly. I can hear."

When Loki comes in, his face lights up at the sight of me horizontal in bed like a regular human being. I tell him how I'll be going to the nursing home for rehab. But then I realize it'll be further away for him—out in the west end of town, they've told me.

"You probably won't come to see me anymore. It'll be too far." I didn't think that would bother me, but it does.

"It's not so far," he says. "Same bus. I just get off it later and get back on earlier."

"So I'll still have to look at your ugly face."

"Yeah." We grin awkwardly at each other. He gives my shoulder a little punch. Then he looks worried. "That didn't hurt you, did it?"

"Take more than you to hurt me."

I tell him what I've decided about my new name. "I'm not Krystal, so don't call me that. My name's Mia now, got it?"

He shakes his head. "What's it with you and names?"

"They have to be right. I'm not Krystal."

"Whatever. Everybody'll think you're weird, though."

The least of my worries.

Susan comes in to see me after supper, and I tell her about going to the other hospital. I don't let on how excited I am. "As soon as my new cast comes in and they get a bed, I'll be going. It could be any day now. The food's supposed to be a lot better."

"That's wonderful!" She reaches over and gives my hand a warm squeeze.

"It's further for Loki to come, but he says he doesn't mind. Is it further for you?"

She gets a funny look on her face. "I'm sorry, Mia, but St. Mary's is with a different board."

"So? What does that mean?"

"I'm afraid I can't see you there."

"What do you mean? They can't keep you out."

Then I get it. She won't get paid for seeing me if I'm at this other hospital. "So you're saying this is, like, just a work thing for you."

"Not at all," she protests. "I know, I'm not happy about it either. But I have to set limits for myself. If I followed all my patients wherever they went, I'd be overwhelmed."

Oh, really? That would be too bad. I don't talk to her after that. I can see she's upset. Good. She gets out her bag and starts shuffling through it. After a while she dumps everything into her lap, glasses case, cellphone, old Kleenexes—until she finds her keys.

Just go.

You don't have to follow them all, I want to say, just me. But all I am is a medical case to her, not a real person. I'm not Krystal, I'm not Amy, and Mia is only a made-up person in my own head.

Just go.

Part II

July

Damage Control

Chapter 7

Once stuff starts happening, it happens fast. A porter shows up to take me down to orthopaedics just when breakfast is being served. When I ask her what it's all about, she doesn't know. Turns out my new plastic body has arrived, and it's time to saw me out of my cast.

The orthopaedic guy holds up the saw with an evil grin. "Let me know if I draw blood." Hospital humour, not funny at all. Before they strap the new cast on, they hose me down again. I don't look—I can't stand it. I try to move my legs a little and stop fast. It hurts like hell.

My breakfast is cold when I get back to my room, something soggy on the tray under a silver lid—a cross between hash browns and a toad. I'm still just looking at it when the nurse bustles in and starts stuffing my things into a bag and tidying up my tubes, catheters, and bags. Don't ask. I'll be going to St. Mary's any minute. "We'll miss you around here," she says. I bet—especially my screaming.

Outside the hospital I get the stretcher guys to stop for a second before they roll me into the ambulance. I want to look at trees without glass between me and them. The leaves are still green—

51

it's only July. They smell fantastic. "Can I have one?" I ask.

They look at each other—*weird*—but then they both pick up a couple of big maple leaves for me. "Have all you want," one says. "They're not going to run out anytime soon."

"Thanks." I clutch them by the stems. They feel waxy, and they have real dirt on them. They feel like summer. I've missed half of it already.

When the stretcher guys wheel me into the new hospital, mostly all I see is a lot of old people. It's a nursing home, right? But they told me people come here to get better, not to die. They only let you in if they think you're going to make it. I'm sharing a room with two white-haired old ladies. When I ask them a bunch of questions about how the place works, they call me "dear." They probably call everybody that, but it's kind of nice.

The window by my bed looks out at a parking lot. I miss the view of the water. Mornings are going to be depressing, not being able to watch the sun come up over the lake. I used to watch out for some sailboat coming down the river and imagine the people on it, wearing clean clothes they just put on, drinking coffee they just made.

My new roommates are both in for broken hips. Phyllis and Evelyn, their names are, but it takes a while to figure out which is which. They both have lots of visitors, and somebody is always asking to borrow my chair. "Help yourself," I say, because no one comes to see me except Loki. I'm still so angry at Susan for deserting me that I can't let myself think about it. All I was to her was a case she got paid to see. For me she was the one person who even tried to understand or believe me about what's happened.

I have to focus instead on what's better here. My new body cast is a huge improvement on the old plaster straitjacket. I've heard they have a pool here somewhere—I can smell chlorine—and the physio says as soon as I get the rest of my casts off, I can swim. I can start to work seriously on this body.

The scary part will be finding out if it works. I can move my legs a little, but I don't know if they'll ever support me. Before the accident I was working so hard to stay in shape for rowing, keeping my weight down without sacrificing muscle. Well, that's all gone now. If I think of that body wasting away now in some hospital in Toronto, I'll go crazy. Look at the mess I'm stuck with instead.

That night I wake up with an image in my head, clear as anything: my backpack sitting on the ground, back from the edge where I dived in the quarry. With my towel and water and sunblock in it— and my cell. Funny, I didn't remember until now.

Where is it now? Mom wouldn't cancel it, that would be too much like saying her daughter wasn't going to make it. Especially when she was in the hospital, "still in very serious condition."

Lying in the dark I imagine myself calling my old number. And *her* answering. I break out into a sweat.

Krystal, this is Amy. Well, actually it's Mia now, but I was Amy before we swapped bodies. Do they call you Amy? Swapping bodies, trading names and lives—there could be a reality show in all this.

The only other person in the whole world beside me who really knows what happened is her. If I'm having trouble with it, she has to be too. She'll want to talk to me. I'm so buzzed at the thought that I can't get back to sleep. I listen to my roommates snore and I wait for the sky to go light. I wonder if Loki will come to see me today. He hasn't been in for a couple of days. And I wonder how I'm going to talk him into bringing me Brittany's sister's phone again.

Hooray, he comes in the afternoon. He's wearing a bright blue scarf—weird. It's July, hardly cold. "It's a Chelsea scarf," he says proudly when I ask what it's about. "Chelsea's my team." Right, but I bet even soccer players don't wear scarves in July. And Loki doesn't play soccer. All he does is skateboard.

"My brother's friend has a flat-screen TV. He gets Gol TV." He goes on about how Chelsea's going to play Barcelona this weekend and get into the European final, or something like that. It's a change from movie plots, but it's not an improvement.

When I can get a word in edgewise, I ask about his brother. "Is he a good guy?"

He snorts. "He's an asshole. He's dying to get a pit bull, but they're illegal. He says he's going to get one anyway. The cops will just take it away and shoot it. And he thinks *I'm* a retard."

I can see why. But then my sister Meaghan never used to think I had much in the way of brains going for me either. She couldn't believe it when I started getting good marks. The thing was, I'd never been motivated before. When I found out that good marks could get me a rowing scholarship to some fantastic place like Washington State, it made sense to try. I have a hunch Loki's the same. It's just that nothing's got him fired up so far.

"Maybe you could go to Europe some day and watch Chelsea play live, not just on TV," I tell him.

He acts like I'm out of my mind. "You can see better on TV. Anyway, where'd I get the money?"

"You'll have a job." He just looks at me and goes back to telling me about this soccer game. Finally I can't wait any longer. "I got this idea, Loki. I could call my own cell in Toronto and talk to her."

"What do you mean, her?"

"Krystal—you know."

He rolls his eyes. "Krystal wouldn't know what to do with a cellphone." Then he catches himself buying into my reality and scowls. "You're nuts. Why are you going on about that stuff for again?"

"I have to try. And you're the only friend I have in the world."

"Brittany's still pissed off. She had to pay her sister six bucks from when you used it. She keeps asking for the money, but I don't have six bucks to throw around. And you've got nothing."

True. I haven't a penny in the world. What can I do to make

him help me? I wonder if I'm going to have to cry.

"Anyway, shut up about it." His voice rises. "You promised you wouldn't talk about it anymore."

"I don't remember promising."

We have a fight in front of the old ladies, and he grabs his stupid scarf and starts to leave. That scares me. He's never done that before. "I'm sorry," I call after him. "Come back. *Please.*"

He stops in the doorway. "Okay," he mutters, "I will. But not now. I gotta go catch the bus. Remember, you promised."

I never promised him anything, damn it. But I need him. Who else is going to visit me? Okay, Krystal's foster mother Joan has come a couple of times and brought me more stuff she thinks I might want. A junky CD player and a bunch of horrible CDs, Goth and rap. Sometimes I listen to them, though, because I think they might tell me something about Krystal. So far all I've learned is the man's gonna get you and it's hard out there for a pimp.

"What happened to those old people?" I ask Joan. I haven't seen them in weeks, maybe even a month.

"Your grandparents, you mean? Your grandfather had an operation."

"Nobody told me."

"First time you've showed any interest."

"What was it for, the operation? Like, cancer, or something serious like that?"

"I don't think so. Men stuff. Plumbing. He's home now, but I told your grandmother not to bother coming to see you. She has enough to worry about, and you never talked to her anyway."

Oh, fine. "Could you please call me Mia?" I say. "Would it kill you?"

Joan sighs. "You were a handful before that accident, but I don't know what to make of you now. You're like a different person."

"That's what I've been telling you. So call me Mia."

Chapter 8

I'm watching *Oprah* with my roommates the next day when a visitor shows up for me, and it's not Loki or Joan.

It's my ex-psychologist Susan. I stare.

"I hope I'm not interrupting anything."

"No." I'm not sure what to say. I suppose she thinks I'm sulking, but I wasn't expecting to see her again. "Are you allowed to come to see me at this hospital now?"

"I'm not here in a professional capacity. Just a visit." She gives a little laugh, and I can see she's nervous. "I've brought you a book." She pulls out a ratty paperback from her bag.

"I can't read very well lately." All the time I was hanging from the ceiling I was dying to read, anything to keep me from going out of my mind. Now that I can actually hold a book and turn the pages, I can't get interested. I tried a couple of mysteries off the book trolley, but they just upset me. You're not supposed to take it seriously when somebody's killed, but it's still death, isn't it? I kept thinking about what happens when you die, and it freaked me out. I have a personal interest in the subject.

"But thanks," I add. *The Blue Castle*, it's called. The cover looks sort of romantic. "I'll try it."

"You'll probably think it's silly and old-fashioned, but it was my favourite book when I was your age. I hope you'll like it. So how are you doing?"

"Great. My catheter's gone," I tell her. "Sorry, that's probably more than you wanted to know."

"That's fantastic, Mia." She smiles like she could really care about my washroom situation.

"And I had a shower. They wrapped my casts in plastic and put me in a wheelchair for it. It was stunningly wonderful. You can have all the bed-baths you like, but you still smell like you're rotting." My mouth seems to have a mind of its own. You'd think I never had a visitor before.

"I'm supposed to get plastic arm casts next week. Then it's just my legs. Then I have to start working on getting from the bed to the wheelchair by myself, and from the wheelchair to the toilet by myself. Then I can start swimming. Then walking. Then I'm out of here."

She laughs. "I see you have an agenda. And you'll do it, too."

"What about you?"

She looks puzzled. "What about me?"

"I mean, how are your kids and everything—if you have kids." I've been thinking since she said she wouldn't be coming anymore that I couldn't blame her for not seeing me as a real person. I mean, I really was just a case. We only talked about me. I never knew anything about her except that she once went to India.

"I don't have children. I do have a partner, and he has children, but they're grown up now. He still worries about them, but I'd say they're doing fine."

"Do you mind not having kids of your own? I mean, if that's not too personal to ask."

"Not at all. I always thought I'd have children, but I never seemed to get around to it. I guess that means I didn't want them very much. I'm happy with the life I have. Usually, anyway."

"Tell me some more about when you lived in India."

She gives me a big smile. "Do you really want to know, or are you being polite?"

"Yeah, I do want to know. About what it was like, you know, every day. What you ate and where you slept and how you brushed your teeth."

She laughs. "We brushed our teeth with a little stick. The fibres at the end were softened so it was like a little paint brush."

She tells me about how she lived in a residence run by nuns. It was in a little village that didn't have running water. They had to get it all from a well. The village didn't have much electricity, just a few light bulbs and they didn't work all the time, just certain hours of the day.

Her eyes go all reminiscent and faraway. "There was another girl from Canada, and two Swiss girls, but most of the others were from India. I wore my hair like they did, darkened it with oil and pulled it back into a bun, painted it red at the part. We wore bright little T-shirt tops and saris. My job was to look after the babies in the orphanage, feed them and play with them. They were very sweet."

I keep asking her questions—not just to be polite. It's interesting. She says she has some pictures somewhere and she'll bring them to show me. Suddenly she looks at her watch. "Look at the time! I didn't mean to stay so long." She starts digging in her big leather bag for her car keys. "Damn, don't tell me I've left them in the car again," she fumes. "Oh, no, here they are!" She holds them up, relieved, and starts dumping everything back in her bag.

Including her cellphone. Of course she has one. I even knew that. Why didn't I think of it before?

"Wait." I take a deep breath and risk it. "Could I use your phone? I need to call long distance, and I can only make local calls here. It's okay, you're allowed to use cellphones in this hospital, as long as it doesn't disturb anybody. I might be able to get some money from my foster mother to pay you."

She's just sitting there, holding the phone in her hand. I see her wanting to ask who I'm going to call.

"I want to call myself. You know. Call my own cell," I tell her. "See if it still works."

"I wondered. I don't think that's a very good idea, Mia. You know what happened the last time."

"You mean, when I called Mom? That was a long time ago. I won't get upset like that now. I've been living with this for months. I just want to find out if the phone's still in service."

"And what if she answers?"

If Krystal answers. "Then I'll talk to her." I hold out my hand. "Please? Please!"

She shakes her head and slips the phone into the bag, out of sight. "I'm late already, Mia. Let me think about it."

"Next time, you promise?"

"No promises. You have to push, don't you?" She sees the look on my face. "But that's good. You wouldn't have got this far otherwise. I'll be back, maybe later this week." She stops in the doorway. "But remember, I'm not promising anything."

Why not? Why the hell not? It's not like she'd be breaking any rules. It might be different if she was still coming to see me as part of her job, though I can't see why. But she came to see me as a friend. What's her problem?

I pick up the book she left me and start to read. It takes me a while to calm down enough to take it in. It's by L.M. Montgomery, the one who wrote *Anne of Green Gables*, but the girl in this book is older. She isn't an orphan, although she doesn't have a father. At first I get excited because it takes place in Muskoka, where our family cottage is. I try to picture where the town might be, but things have probably changed a lot since the time the book was written.

Susan's right—*The Blue Castle* is corny. But on the other hand it doesn't upset me. I don't get too far with it before dinner, but I go back to it afterwards. It makes the time pass, and there must be something in it that made Susan like it. A message she wants me to get.

The next time Krystal's foster mother comes to see me, I bring up the subject of what's going to happen when I get out of the hospital.

Joan looks uncomfortable. "I need to talk to you about that. I can't take you back, Krystal. You always were a handful, but we managed. And I'll give you credit—you were good with the young ones. Paige has been acting up ever since you've been in the hospital. But you need somebody who can look after you. I can't do that. I'm run off my feet as it is. Half the time I feel I can't look after the kids I've got."

I don't think I'd want to go and live with Joan anyway. It sounds like a zoo. "What's going to happen to me, then? I can't stay here forever."

"They may have to find you a group-home situation. Nobody's been to see you about that?"

Nope, not so far as I know. They probably figured I'd die and wouldn't be a problem. Maybe Susan was supposed to look after it. Or maybe I saw a social worker in the big hospital and I've just forgotten. It's all foggy.

"What about my mother? Would she take me?" If she lives in Windsor, that's closer to Toronto.

Joan presses her lips together. "I don't think that's a good idea, honey. She still has that same boyfriend."

I get a bad feeling when she says that. Something's going on there. I don't explore it. Anyway, from what I've heard of Krystal's mother, she's a write-off.

Who else is there? Susan won't even lend me her cellphone—I'm sure she wouldn't want me in her house. "What about those grandparents? Couldn't I live with them?"

"They don't need any more trouble. They're old. You gave them hell when you lived with them before."

I lived with them before? News to me. "When was that?"

"Before you ended up with me."

"Well, I don't know anything about that, but they don't have to worry. I'm different now."

She shakes her head.

"Could you at least ask them for me?" I'm pleading.

Chapter 9

"I've been thinking that what's happened to me, this body-switch thing, is kind of like time travel," I tell Susan the next time she comes.

She goes all wary. She's not too comfortable with this stuff. Supposing it's true? What's she going to do about it? She's embarrassed she's buying into it.

"You know, like in those books where people get transported to the French Revolution or Sherwood Forest. One minute they're lying in their bed, and the next they're sitting around some campfire in the Middle Ages. Except that what happened to me is travel in the same time but to another body."

"But that's fantasy," Susan reminds me. "Fiction. Tales of imagination."

"Yeah, but writers *thought* of it. So maybe things like that have actually happened."

"No, Mia. You can't switch brains between bodies. Brain and body aren't two systems, they're one. Inseparable. Everything we've learned about the brain tells us that memory is laid down chemically and electrically in our cells through what we experience. If you have Krystal's body, you have her brain and her memories.

Nothing else is possible. I'm sorry."

Huh. But now that I think of it, maybe I do have some shadowy things in my brain that seem to belong more to Krystal than me. Not much, just a sense I might have known something before, like déjà vu but about something that Amy couldn't possibly know. Like, when Joan mentioned Krystal's mother's boyfriend, I got a sick feeling in my stomach. And, like, there's some connection between Loki and me. I didn't get it at the first, but I do now.

I back up a bit. "When you die, your brain's gone too, right? The memory goes away. If they don't get you started up again fast, you're a vegetable. The brain doesn't have anything in it. But where did all those memories go?"

"Once they're gone, they're gone, as far as I know. Brain-dead, they call it. Like a dead hard drive."

"But that's not what happened to me. My hard drive shut down, but it didn't get thrown away. It got recycled and when it came back up, it was in a different machine."

"That only makes sense if someone switched your hard drives," Susan says. "If you had an actual, physical brain transplant. If such a thing were possible, which it isn't."

"Or, the hard drives wouldn't have to be switched." I'm getting excited. "All the data could be sent across, like over the Internet. Like downloading songs from somebody else's computer."

She shakes her head like there's a fly buzzing around it. "I don't know how we got into computer analogies. I'm hopeless with technology."

Well, she was the one that brought it up.

"Maybe a way of approaching this is multiple personality syndrome," she says. "Several personalities existing in the same psyche. It's a phenomenon that's been studied and documented." She feels on safer ground now, I can tell.

"How does that happen?"

"Usually there's been some sort of psychological trauma.

Sexual abuse or extreme cruelty. To be able to stand to go on living, the person has to shut off the old identity and create another one. The curious thing is that sometimes these people have complex memories of other 'lives' that are very puzzling. It's hard to imagine how they could have invented them, based on their own experience. Like your very detailed accounts of Toronto life."

"Did you check them out?"

"Some things," she admits.

I don't like her multiple-personality-syndrome idea much. I don't feel multiple. "What about the soul?" I ask. Once before, she said something about the human spirit.

"Ah," she says, "the soul."

I figured with her India experience, that would mean something to her. "Reincarnation," I prompt. "There's millions of people who believe in that. My soul started out its journey in one body and when it died—sort of—it went into another."

She looks thoughtful, but I can't get anything more out of her. However it happened, possible or not, it's happened, and I'm living with it. The thing is, what can I do about it? I don't know how I'm going to get out of this body and back into my right one. At least not yet.

And in the meantime, what am I going to do about this pitiful wreck?

The next time I see my doctor, I ask about growth hormones. At least I think he's my doctor, since I've seen him more than twice in a row. He's quite young and looks Asian but he doesn't have any accent.

"No need for those," he says. "You're within the normal range."

"I think I'm going to be shorter than I was. Because of the accident."

"The X-rays don't show any spinal compression. The fear was

that with the trauma to your spine, the spinal cord could be damaged. You were immobilized to allow it to heal. That was done by putting you in traction, so you wouldn't lose any height in the process."

"When my spine is healed, I will be able to walk, won't I?" I sound casual, but I'm terrified of the answer.

"We can't rush it. You can feel sensation and you can move your legs—all positive. We'll wait and see." He's not giving out any guarantees.

"Wouldn't growth hormones help with the healing?"

"No." You can't suggest anything to a doctor, even a young one. "Anyway, you likely haven't stopped growing. You're only fifteen."

"I'm sixteen."

"Fifteen." He shows me my chart. He's right. It says Krystal was born August 29, fifteen years ago. But I was sixteen, nearly seventeen when I had the accident. My birthday's in June. Funny, I just thought we'd be the exact same age. Like the universe would say, "Two Geminis: perfect match. Switch!"

Once I'm over the shock of that, I think, well, if this body is only fifteen, maybe there's hope. In health class in my old school, we saw a video once about three generations of one family. The grandparents were like little gnomes, like Krystal's, the parents sort of normal, and the kids giants. All because of nutrition. It's a bit late for nutrition to kick in now, but it's all I have. Besides, it's something I know about from rowing. Nutrition is crucial for building muscle.

I complain so much about the food I'm getting that they get the dietician to come and talk to me. When she turns up, she looks about twenty. I don't know if that's good or bad. "I need a lot more protein than I'm getting," I tell her. "The meals here have way too many carbs."

"You need carbs," she says primly.

"Complex, not refined ones. The vegetables here are awful, all the life cooked out of them. I bet not a single vitamin survives. The raw vegetables are just as bad—iceberg lettuce! That's just water!"

If looks could kill, I'd be dead. "Your family is welcome to supplement your diet."

"I don't have a family. I only have a foster mother, and she can't afford to bring me stuff. And I don't have any money of my own." Start the violins—I sound so pitiful my own eyes well up.

She presses her lips together, but we make a deal. Whole-grain bread, fish three times a week, lots of eggs, apples, bananas. All the yogourt I want.

"Not so much sugar," I tell her. "No white flour. I don't see how you get away with feeding things like that to sick people."

"Most people here like the food. If I cut those things out, I'd have a riot on my hands."

"And everything organic, right?" I call after her. "That's very important for sick people."

She doesn't even turn around.

Susan says she's been talking to Joan about going after the driver of the truck to get an insurance settlement. Joan doesn't have the time or energy to take it on, but Susan says somebody should, and soon. She knows a lawyer who will take on my case, for a cut of whatever we get. If he doesn't win, he won't get anything. "Are you okay with going ahead on that basis?" she asks me.

What have I got to lose? Krystal doesn't have any money for lawyers. "Ask for a million."

"He thinks we should be able to get $75,000 without much problem. The driver was charged with reckless driving and not giving way to pedestrians. But it was partly your fault, you know. You walked into the intersection without looking."

"Krystal's fault. *She* didn't look."

"Whatever we get will go into a trust fund for rehabilitation and education," Susan says.

"Would rehabilitation include plastic surgery?" I could have liposuction on Krystal's roly-poly thighs.

"That's one thing we don't have to worry about. You're very lucky not to have much facial scarring."

"It's not the scars, it's the face." I'm thinking about how I could get this face to look like my old one.

"The face is fine. A very nice one." Susan hunts in her big bag and pulls out a lipstick with a little mirror on the side, frowning into it. "When you get old, you get these lines, and the lipstick runs into them. I remember when I was a kid, all my mother's bridge friends were like that. I can't believe it's happening to me."

"So get collagen injections. My mother does. One of my friends got them in her lips. She looked like she got hit with a hockey puck."

"I've thought of getting a face lift," Susan admits. "But then you see those women at the Hollywood award shows—they're really eighty, but they've had so many lifts their faces don't look like any age at all. But the way they move gives them away. They look like eighty-year-olds wearing masks."

"It might work for me, though."

"Seriously, I don't think that's a very good idea, Mia."

"About your cellphone," I remind her. "Can I use it?"

She shakes her head.

Chapter 10

By now I'm absolutely frantic to get out of plaster. Finally they replace everything with removable plastic, except for my right leg, which was really badly smashed. That's still in plaster from my hip to my knee. Even when it comes off, I'll have to wear a brace.

But at least now I can go in a wheelchair down to the sunroom. I'm supposed to be pushed, though. I'm not allowed to wheel myself yet, because my wrists are still healing. That means I hardly ever get to go anywhere. When the nurses take me, they park me and forget to come back.

"Couldn't I get an electric one with controls where you just move a lever?" I ask.

Phyllis in the next bed clicks her tongue at Evelyn. "Girl wants the moon."

"Just write them a cheque, honey," says Evelyn. "Ask the nurses to pick you up one at Wal-Mart."

When Loki comes in, I get him to help me into the wheelchair. He's strong—all that skateboarding has to be good for something. I put my arms around his neck so he can lift me. He's got his head in my cleavage. "Hey, don't get any ideas," I say.

"Wouldn't be the first time," he mutters as I drop into the wheelchair.

What?

"Say that again."

"It wouldn't be the first time." He straightens up. His eyes connect with mine, then slide away. He's not great at eye contact.

Oh, no. Phyllis and Evelyn are listening with interest. "Push me outside," I say.

After he wheels me out and around the hospital, we get to a spot under the trees where I can see Lake Ontario in the distance, just a bit of blue between the branches. "Stop here."

He does, but he stays behind me, where I can't see him. "So what are you trying to tell me?" I ask.

"What do you mean?"

I twist around to look him in the eye. "I mean, were we, did we—?" I can't say it.

"Yeah."

Oh no! How disgusting! I can't even bear to look at him, zits and hoodie and eleven-hair moustache. That little slut Krystal! She was probably giving blowjobs in the parking lot at school dances too.

He pulls his skateboard out of his pack and heads to the front steps of the hospital. I stare towards the water and think how Krystal's love life was light years away from what Nate and I had together. Or could have had.

Loki jumps off the hospital steps about fifty times until somebody comes out and yells at him to cut it out. It was getting on my nerves too.

"So just what exactly did we do?" I ask when he's back within speaking distance.

"You know."

"I don't, which is why I'm asking. Were we drunk?"

"Uh, yeah, I guess. Sort of." He paws the ground with one foot.

"And what exactly happened?"

He doesn't want to talk about it, but I get it out of him. There was this party, bunch of fourteen- and fifteen-year-olds, big bottle of hard stuff—gin, rye, whatever—made up out of shots stolen from their parents' liquor cabinets. Krystal has too much to drink and starts crying about her life. She's just moved into foster care after being thrown out of her grandparents' place. She's already been thrown out of her home after her mother's boyfriend kept coming on to her, and when she complained about it, her mother got mad at *her*—said it was her fault, the way she dressed. Brittany and the other girls made her go to the school guidance counsellor, and then her mother really got mad at her. So now she's got no family to turn to, she's bawling her eyes out, Loki puts his arms around her, and one thing leads to another.

I can't believe this. "You mean the poor kid's upset about being sexually molested by some creep and kicked out of her home, and then *you* molest her?"

He glowers. "That was a year before, that other stuff. And it wasn't like that, like you make it sound. We were only, uh—you know."

"I'm telling you, I *don't* know. I'm asking. Was there sex? Was or was there not penetration?"

"Shut up!" Loki looks around nervously.

"Tell me! Was there or wasn't there?"

"Not exactly, okay?" He clenches his fists and his face turns red. "Shut up about it. Don't talk like that. And stop talking that way about *her*. It was *you*."

"Ha! Even if it was, how would I remember? I was drunk, wasn't I?"

We glare at each other. He turns away and picks up his board and stuffs it into his pack. He's going to take off and leave me.

"Oh, don't go." Nobody uses this entrance anymore. I could be stuck here for hours.

After all, he's just a boy. What do I expect?

To be honest, I don't have a lot of sexual experience myself. I was always too busy training. Technically, I'm not a virgin, although I doubt the guy involved would be able to recall. He was a big rowing hotshot and I was his date at a party and I thought that was what I had to do to get respect. The whole event was pretty horrible, and I decided I wouldn't do it again until I found someone I loved. And when I finally found someone I could love, I didn't get a chance to do anything about it.

Anyway, Loki and Krystal were just kids. As long as he doesn't still have any ideas in that regard. "Let's just forget it. Look." I swivel my ankles around. All Loki sees is hairy legs sticking out of pyjamas, so that's not exactly going to get him hot. "I can move them. They work. I'm getting the last of the plaster off on Monday. Maybe by the time school starts, I'll be walking. On crutches, anyway."

He sulks for a while before he finally says something. "You want to go to *school*?"

"It'll be a lot less boring than lying around here all day."

He swears under his breath. Loki's not the academic type.

I'm working with the physio, getting stronger every day. There's so much to do before I can leave here. Joan said she's asked the grandparents if they'll take me, but they haven't said yes or no. Probably just stared at her, horrified. Well, at least that's not a no. If they do agree to take me, and I haven't given up hoping yet, I know they won't be able to lift me or anything. I'll have to be absolutely able to look after myself. I'm working on it as hard as I can.

Monday the last of the plaster comes off. Tuesday I get to swim for the first time. It's humiliating being in a bathing suit with big boobs and hairy legs. But when we start getting close to the pool, my nostrils twitch, scenting that chlorine. The next best thing to being in a boat is being in the water.

Annie the physio transfers me to a bath chair and lowers me into the water. I float. It feels heavenly, blood warm, a rush. I want to dive out of her arms and power my way to the end of the pool, leaving her in my wake. I kick, but this body doesn't know what to do. My legs churn sluggishly.

"Easy, easy." Annie reins me in. "Not so fast. One leg at a time. That must hurt."

It does, but I'm not telling her. It doesn't hurt much. Even after what happened at the quarry, I feel like once I'm in water I'm safe, even though I'm being carried creaking from one end of the pool to the other, cradled in Annie's arms.

"Had enough for one day?" she asks.

"No!"

We go up and down the pool one more time, and then she wants to get out. "Just a little longer," I beg. She gets me a kick-board and lets me stay in another five minutes.

It's the oddest sensation, my brain knowing what to do but my body acting like playdough. And I admit, by the time Annie gets me dried off and into my chair again and back to my room, I'm like a limp rag. I sleep straight through lunch. When I wake up I can hardly move, my muscles are so stiff.

But in a good way.

Every day I'm closer to getting out of this joint. Joan keeps talking about the dreaded group home. I keep nagging her to ask Krystal's grandparents if they've decided to take me.

"Against my better judgment," she says. "Two old people and a fifteen-year-old girl? Seems to me like a recipe for disaster. They haven't got a chance."

But a couple of days later she comes in with the old lady trailing behind her. I hold my breath for the worst but, thank heavens, it's a go. They'll have to make changes to the house, Joan says, but they're willing. She's trying to find out for them if there's a disability allowance to help them do it.

"You're a lucky girl, Krystal, after everything that's happened," she mutters close to my ear. I can see she doesn't mean my accident. "If you break their hearts, you'll answer to me."

"She's a good girl," says the grandmother, patting my arm. Well, I am, but that's because I'm not Krystal.

Anyway, the old lady is on Krystal's side, and as far as I can see, Krystal doesn't have that many allies. I think of my own real family—Mom, Dad, Gillian and Meaghan, Aunt Barb and Aunt Marianne, Grandma and Grandpa Mackenzie on Dad's side and Gran Albrecht and her boyfriend on Mom's side. All the cousins. Money? No worries. Christmas? Let's everybody fly down to St Bart's. That really happened once. Amazing.

Part III

August

Impostor

Chapter 11

In the first week of August I leave the hospital to move to the grandparents' house—Ava and Avo, I'm supposed to call them. I'm excited. Phyllis and Evelyn and the nurses give me a silly good-bye card they've signed. I know I should be grateful for all everybody's done for me, but I can't get out of there fast enough.

Joan comes to help get me and my things into the access vehicle. We drive down shady streets of stone mansions, and then the streets start getting narrower. The driver has a little trouble locating the place. "James Street is just off Pine," Joan tells him. Apparently it's not one of the better-known addresses.

The van pulls up in front of a row of mean little houses. I spot Loki sitting on his skateboard on the sidewalk. Two old people come out the front door. I guess this is the place.

It's a narrow white house. The only thing that makes it any different from the other houses is it has tomatoes and flowers where the others have scabby bits of front lawn. The driver lowers my wheelchair to the sidewalk and hauls out three plastic bags. They're all I own in the world, except for some other grimy Goth junk Joan says she's brought over here from her house.

The grandfather is frowning. He has the biggest ears I've ever seen on a human being. The grandmother is rubbing her hands nervously. "This way," she says, and leads everybody around the side of the house, like a parade. There's a brand-new ramp going up to the back door, not even painted.

"We build this for you," she says and looks at me solemnly. What am I supposed to say? I can't seem to talk.

I get a glimpse of the backyard: wall-to-wall tomatoes. The wheelchair just makes it through the back door, an inch to spare. Loki pushes, Joan directs.

"This is your room," the grandmother says, backing down the hall in front of us and pointing. "The bathroom is so near, next door."

Why did I think this was a good idea? Everything is hideous. The window has yellow vertical blinds—vertical!—and they're drawn tight shut. Haven't these people heard of Ikea? Pictures of Jesus with his heart exposed, Mary with glass tears. The room smells mothballs. No bedside lamp, just a dim bulb in the ceiling.

I look at this strange old couple who are supposed to be my grandparents. They look back at me. "They've gone to a lot of trouble," Joan hisses. "You could at least say thanks."

"Thank you," I say. "I really appreciate your taking me. It means a lot to me." It doesn't come out sounding sincere.

"The mattress we buy new," the old lady says proudly.

I lurch out of the wheelchair to the bed. It's hard as rock. It also crinkles. There's a plastic cover on it so I won't pee or bleed on it and spoil it. "I'm really tired," I say. I really am, and I can't bear another minute of this life I'm in. I close my eyes.

"I gotta go," I hear Loki mutter.

I sit up on one elbow in alarm. "Will you come back? Take me for a walk?"

"Sure."

I lie down again.

"She doesn't have much energy yet," Joan says. Pretty soon I hear the door shut and muffled voices in the hall. Then it's quiet.

I'm so miserable, I wish I'd died back at the start. I don't know what I expected when I got out of the hospital, but I never thought it would be a dark little hole with a couple of weird old people for prison guards. "Mommy, Mommy, come and get me," I moan into the pillow. I haven't called her mommy for a long time.

But you can only cry so long before you get sick of it. I know this move has got to work. I don't have any other choices. There's a box of tissues by the bed and I mop my face and blow my nose until the tears dry up. This is not forever. When I'm stronger, I'll figure out what to do. I've always been good at solving problems, working out how to get what I want. I'll find a way to get back to me.

I've blown my nose raw when there's a teeny-tiny knock on the door. It's the grandmother, Ava. "I made you some nice lunch," she says. But she isn't carrying a tray or anything. "You come."

I get the idea. I flop out into the wheelchair and roll down the hall after her, grazing my knuckles on the door frame. There's one place set at the kitchen table, scratched green top with aluminum legs. She's made me a big sandwich.

"I'm not very hungry."

She folds her arms, standing beside me. "You must eat to get better."

"What about you and, uh, Avo?"

"We ate," she says. "It's two o'clock." She sounds scandalized at the time.

The sandwich is dark and sour-looking, with a dill pickle. I never liked dill pickles. But once I take a bite, I remember the last time I ate anything was before seven this morning. I eat it all. Ava is nodding her head. "Good, good." She pushes a glass of milk towards me. It tastes delicious, obviously not skim. I'm going to have to watch it or I'll get fat as a pig, dumpy little Krystal all over again.

"Here is Avo."

The old man comes in from the backyard and drops a bunch of dirty vegetables in the sink—beets, I think. He says something in another language. Then he takes a glass of brownish liquid from the counter, drains it, and goes back out to the garden.

I can't help asking. "Was that beer?"

Ava shakes her head, startled. "No, no. Tea."

Cold tea? More weirdness. But better than what I thought, which was that Avo was some kind of alcoholic. "Joan says he had an operation. Is he okay?"

She nods soberly. "Yes. He is back in his garden, thanks be to God. Otherwise he is impossible."

When I ask if I can use the phone to call Loki, I see a worried look cross her face. "Your mother, when she lives here, she was also one for the phone. Talking, talking all the time."

"Don't worry, I'm not going to be phoning much. I've only got one friend."

Obviously if Krystal's mother lived here too, they've been in this house for a thousand years. "When did my mother leave here?" I ask. "Was that before I was born? Sorry, I can't remember things very well since the accident."

She twists her hands. "After. Then your mother takes you away."

I work out that Krystal and her mother both lived here when Krystal was a baby. Krystal's mother was young when she got married, only seventeen. Her husband wasn't much older. I guess he got fed up living with her parents and a baby and took off. Krystal and her mother stayed on a couple years more.

"But your Avo, he doesn't like all the boyfriends she has. She was very angry with us. We hardly see you any more. My poor little girl."

Krystal and her mom get their own place, which is fine until Krystal gets older and her mother's boyfriend, or boyfriends, start noticing Krystal. Then she goes back to live with her grandparents, but that doesn't last long. She's acting out, talking back, staying out late, and they can't handle her, so she ends up in foster care. I guess they felt bad about it, though.

"I know that if I give you any trouble, I won't be allowed to stay," I assure her. "You don't need to worry." But I can see why she might be worried.

This morning when we were leaving the hospital, Joan said to me, "Don't forget you're on probation, Krystal."

Yeah, right. They've built that huge ramp to the back door and they're going to throw me out the first time I get out of line? I don't think so. "My name's Mia," I said back. Joan never remembers. "Call me Mia, okay? Anyway, you don't need to tell me. I'm different now."

"That's what you always say."

"But it's me saying it now, not Krystal."

Now I ask Ava, "Could you call me Mia, not Krystal, please?" I say it extremely politely.

She furrows her wrinkly forehead. "Why I should do that?"

I know nobody likes people changing their names. It seems like a flaky thing to do. There was this guy at my old school, Todd, who changed his name to Tristan. Tristan! You can imagine the shit he got for that.

"I don't want to be rude, Ava, but I don't like the name. I don't feel like Krystal anymore."

"Krystiana Maria Marques." Or I think that's what she says.

"Pardon?"

"Krystiana Maria Marques," she repeats. "Your name, how you were christened. It was your mother called you Krystal."

Interesting bit of information. "So—are you okay with calling me Mia?"

She shrugs. "Mia, Krystal." Then she smiles. "When you were a baby, I call you Mimi. So Mia is no problem, I guess."

Mia Marques? A little too much alliteration, but it could be lots worse.

The phone rings after supper around eight o'clock. I'm in my bedroom. The grandparents are in the living room watching television. It's for me. I have to get into the wheelchair and roll out to the phone. They don't even have a cordless. Ava turns the television down.

The only person I can think it would be is Loki. But it isn't, it's a woman's voice. "So how are you getting along?" It's Susan!

"Fine." What else am I going to say with the old folks sitting beside me?

"I just thought you might be feeling a little glum. It can be a bit of a letdown, getting out of the hospital. Like a lot of things we really look forward to."

Her kind, gentle voice makes me want to start bawling. "I'm okay. My grandparents fixed up a room for me and everything." And they're two feet away from me.

"I'm sorry I haven't been able to get in to see you lately. Maybe we can go shopping on the weekend, get you some new things for school. Would you like that?"

Sure, although I have no idea what I'm going to use for money. The thought of getting out does cheer me up.

"Just let me know when you're ready," she says. "Give me a call."

After I hang up, I wonder if the grandparents are mad at me for talking on their phone. But Ava only says, "That was a nice lady."

Chapter 12

I spend next morning figuring out how to make my bed, how to take a shower and get dressed. That takes two hours. Then I call Loki and get him to say he'll come over to see me. He can't come till the afternoon. After lunch I manage to open the back door and wheel myself down the ramp so I can sit under the one tree in the yard. It's hot even in the shade.

I watch Avo working in the sun, weeding and weeding, red suspenders straining over his bent back. He doesn't make eye contact or say anything to me. His tomatoes are weird looking, dark purple and yellow, pink ones big as a baby's head. I've never seen tomatoes like that.

When Loki shows up around two, I'm desperate to get away. "Can we go down to the water from here?" I beg.

He has to think about it. "I guess so."

It turns out to be only three blocks or so, a wide river or bay. There's like a medieval fort or something on the other side, stone towers with red roofs, very old looking and romantic. Ducks, seagulls, sailboats. And he never comes down here! "I'd come here all the time," I say.

"We used to come and hunt for turtles and things, me and my

brother. But that's kid stuff. It's no good for swimming or nothing." The water looks weedy and shallow. He points to a bridge in the distance. "You can swim over there. You're not supposed to, but a lot of guys jump off the bridge."

It looks high. A shiver goes through me.

Loki pushes me along a path by the shore with willows overhanging it. A couple of middle-aged women jog past. An old guy walks a fluffy little dog. And then right ahead of us I see a big shed with a sign on the side: Cataraqui Rowing Club. My heart lurches.

"You never told me there was a rowing club!"

"Big deal. Didn't know there was one."

Well, I did, actually, because our club used to row against it. But I forgot. "Push me over!" But when we're closer I see the building is all closed up, and there are no windows to peer in.

I'll come back. I'm already feeling happier, knowing I'm only a couple of blocks from a river and a rowing club. We continue along the path, and I ask Loki about soccer. He tells me how well Chelsea is doing and how they have a Portuguese coach now. It's the same as when he talks about movies: Once he gets going, it's like having the radio on.

I think of something I meant to ask and interrupt him. "So where's the school? The one I'll be going to?"

"Regi? You still got amnesia? It's up there." He points.

"How many blocks from where I live?"

"Close. Four, maybe?"

Not far, but more than I can manage in a wheelchair. "I'll have to practise with my crutches." Except I can't imagine lasting a whole day on crutches and hobbling home at the end of it.

"I can take you. Wheel you there."

"Would you really?" I turn and stare at him in surprise. I didn't think he'd want to. I thought he'd be embarrassed. "You won't have to do it for long. Just at the beginning, until I get stronger."

"Doesn't matter. Nothin' better to do."

Next morning I call the school and talk to the secretary. She gives me an appointment right away with a guidance counsellor, that same afternoon. Loki pushes me there and hangs around outside with his skateboard until I'm done.

The school isn't the dump I was afraid it would be. No girls in micro-kilts in sight. From the outside it looks old, kind of like a castle, set way back from the street behind a huge green sports field. But inside everything feels cheerful and new: the floors gleam and the walls and locker doors have a fresh coat of bright chilli-red paint. Everything smells like it's just been cleaned.

The counsellor's name is Mr. Mallen. He's my dad's age but less cool and more out of shape. Podgy face, hair with bangs like Spock from *Star Trek*, Birkenstocks, with socks.

"What can we do for you, Krystal?" he asks, not very friendly.

"I appreciate your seeing me on short notice," I say politely. "It's nice of you to come in while it's still summer vacation."

"I wouldn't be here if they weren't paying me."

Oh. Right. Good to know. "I've kind of lost track of things since my accident," I tell him. "Could you show me the marks I got for last year?"

"They were sent out in June. You must have received them."

"I used to be in foster care, and I'm not anymore. I'm living with my grandparents now. I guess the envelope must have got lost."

He sighs like it's my fault. Taking a transcript from a fat folder with my name on it, he shoves it across the desk. My palms get clammy as I reach for it.

Yikes. The marks are just as bad as I was afraid of. English is the only one over 60, and it's just 72.

"Your teachers all passed you, even though English was the only subject you were doing well in. They gave you a break because of your accident. Pardon the pun."

Can you believe that? My mouth drops open. He's joking about the accident! That's not very nice, especially for a counsellor. He's supposed to be supportive. Poor Krystal got wiped out by a truck, and he's making a pun out of it? She could have died or been paralyzed for life. I push the rest of that thought away.

He's started going on about all the classes Krystal skipped. I cut him off when he takes a breath. "That isn't going to happen any more," I say. "I want to know what I have to do to graduate."

"Graduate?" He peers at me over his glasses. "You have two more years before you finish the baccalaureate program."

Two more years! At my old school I only had one. Two more years of high school! I'll never last.

I take a deep breath and make my voice as steady as I can. "I need to find out what courses I'll be taking this fall so that I can get the books ahead of time. I want to get started early because of all the school you say I missed. Anyway, I don't have anything else to do for the next few weeks."

He blinks, and his mouth opens. I keep on talking. "I've been thinking about it. I need really good marks. If the insurance money for the accident doesn't come through, I'll need a scholarship if I want to go to university."

"University?" Now he's incredulous. I don't tell him the university needs to be U of T. He clears his throat, like he's shifting gears. "I'm glad to see some good has come from the accident," he says gruffly. "It's obviously made you see you can't go on the way you were."

What a jerk this guy is. But I leave with a stack of books for math, politics, and French. A bunch more for English including *To Kill a Mockingbird* and *Julius Caesar*, which I already studied. Piece of cake.

Loki pushes me home again. "What've you got all that crap for?"

"For getting on with life. Like you should be doing, unless you want to be stuck in this dump of a town forever."

"Why do you have to be so friggin' high and mighty about everything? You never used to be like that."

"Like, in the good old days, smoking, and getting wasted with you, you mean? I guess I used to be a lot more interesting."

He doesn't answer for a minute. "I wouldn't exactly say that," he says.

When I get home there's a letter on the kitchen table, addressed to Krystal. No return address. Ava hovers, trying not to look like she's dying of curiosity. Inside there's a funny card with a chicken, the kind adults buy about how awful birthdays are. It's signed "Mom."

Not my mom. Krystal's.

Ava is very busy at the stove, but watching me out of the corner of her eye. I wheel my chair around and give her the card. "When's my birthday?"

Her hand flies to her mouth. "Oh! Your birthday!"

"You know how I forget everything, Ava, even my birthday. Because of my amnesia." That's what we're calling it.

"I forget too!" she cries. There are tears in her eyes. "Yesterday it was your birthday, and I forget. We both forget. What a pair!" She leans down and hugs me. She smells vinegary, like sweet relish.

Krystal's mother remembered and sent a card (late). Too busy to call, though. Not that I'd want to talk to her anyway. "I'm sixteen, right, Ava?"

"Sweet sixteen." She bustles to the cupboards, taking down the canisters of flour and sugar. "I make a cake."

"I don't need a cake, but thanks."

"No cake? Yes, cake. You must have cake!"

"Putrid cake," I think she calls it. That can't be right. I can't figure out if that's the Portuguese word or not. Anyway, it sure isn't putrid—it has honey and mint and orange in it. It's supposed to have whipped cream on top, but I ask her to leave it off mine.

When we sit down to supper, there's a present by my plate, a chocolate bar with foreign writing.

"From Belgium," says Avo gruffly. "The best chocolate in the world they make."

"Thanks very much, Avo." I open it to share.

But neither of them will take any. "No, no. That is all for you," Avo says. "The birthday girl."

I don't tell them I'm not eating chocolate until I get down to my target weight. Loki loves chocolate—I'll give it to him. I mean, it's really very kind of them, but all of a sudden I feel depressed.

My real birthday was on June 19. Gemini, sign of the heavenly twins—how ironic. I missed it completely, didn't even know what day it was. On my sixteenth birthday, last year, we all went out for dinner to a place called Fred's Not Here—Mom, me, Meaghan, Meaghan's brand-new baby, Stacey, and Meaghan's husband (she has one of those too). Dad dropped in for dessert *sans* girlfriend and gave me a cheque. Afterwards I went out with my fake ID and friends. I couldn't drink, of course, because I was in training, but I had a fabulous time.

Chapter 13

I'm all for throwing out the bags of Krystal's things that Joan brought over, but Ava hunts through them and finds a school uniform. The skirt is as short as the ones on those girls who came to see me in the hospital.

I don't know how to sew, but I could rip out the big black stitches in the hem. The problem then would be the raw, jagged edge. "Can you fix it for me?" I beg Ava. She's an old woman. Old women know how to sew.

She takes the skirt from me and clucks her tongue. "Why you cut this off so ragged, stupid girl?" But she can't turn me down for wanting to dress more respectably. She has a good idea to sew a strip of material along the bottom to turn up for the hem. If I wear knee socks, the scars on my legs will be covered. She washes all my uniform shirts and bleaches out the stains. Then she sews buttons on them so I don't have to go to school with major cleavage.

Every morning and again in the afternoon I drag myself up and down the concrete block paths between Avo's garden rows. Twenty times, thirty times, forty times around on my crutches with my leg brace, until I'm dripping from the pain and the heat. I also try to walk by pushing my wheelchair as a support. Only two weeks until school, and I can hardly balance on one crutch without my legs giving way.

Then it's only ten days before school starts. How am I ever going to get strong enough to manage? Then I remember I can swim, at least sort of, and that might help. I call Loki and ask him to take me to the local pool.

"Costs money," he objects.

"I'll pay." My grandparents have started giving me an allowance out of what they get for taking care of me: I have fifteen dollars a week and nowhere to spend it.

"I guess I could try out the weights," Loki says.

But I make him go into the pool. I need him to help me into the water. He comes out of the men's dressing room wearing huge shorts and a big t-shirt. The only thing he's taken off are his shoes.

"Where's your suit?"

"Don't need one."

"Your body can't be that terrible, with all the boarding you do."

He dips his head. Does he even have a suit? Turns out he's afraid of water.

"You can't *swim*?"

"Shut up." He glares.

I shut up. Hell, he can't swim—I can barely crawl. And also, when you think about it, somebody has to teach you to swim. Somebody you trust. From what Loki's told me about his mother, she probably never gets any closer to water than the bathroom.

"You won't have to get wet above your waist," I promise. "Just help me in the shallow end." He lifts me from the wheelchair and lowers me onto the side of the pool. "Careful, don't drop me!" But he's strong. Of course, I'm not that heavy anymore.

I grab the ladder. "Get us a couple of kickboards, would you?"

"Not for me. I'm not going in there."

"Fine. Just one."

I churn up and down the pool, between the bobbing, pink-faced oldies and blue-lipped kids shivering in their parents' arms. Loki waits by the edge of the pool, arms crossed, looking bored.

It's three visits before I finally coax him into the water and get him to take his feet off the bottom. He grips the kickboard, his teeth clenched, white showing around his eyeballs.

"Kick!"

He kicks so hard I can't see him through the splashing. I follow in his wake. He bumps into the end of the pool and holds on to the side, rubbing his skull. His hair drips. "I did it." He sounds amazed. "Wasn't so bad."

Pretty good, actually.

Between studying to get ready for school and trying to get stronger, I'm wiped every night by suppertime. I help Ava with the dishes—there's no dishwasher!—and then wheel myself to my room and plug myself into Krystal's old Discman. I've got a CD that Loki gave me by some local technopunk band called Metrognome. I don't like it much but it beats Krystal's Goth stuff.

As far as the room goes, I haven't been able to do much with it, but I've opened the blinds and the window, so it smells less like mothballs. It's not like anybody can see in, because there's a tall fence outside with lilacs behind. When the sun goes down, the leaves are shot through with golden light.

I'd like to take down the religious pictures, but I don't want to get on the old people's bad side. I've decided I can live with Jesus and Mary. Both of them knew what it was like to have a secret, I guess, to live a reality so different from everybody else's that if you told anybody, they'd lock you up. Did Mary tell her friends about Jesus' father being God, not Joseph? I bet she didn't. I bet she told Jesus to keep that stuff quiet at school.

Jesus is smiling down at me from the foot of the bed, his heart in his hand. "Don't you have a T-shirt you can put on?" I scold him. "You're going to get a terrible chest cold like that."

I'm usually on my way to sleep before Ava and Avo have gone to bed, and they're not exactly creatures of the night. Actually, they're early risers, but one morning I wake up so early they're still out for the count. The clock by my bed says just six. The sky is blue and clear. It's a perfect morning and I have an idea.

Quiet as I can, I pull on jeans and a T-shirt. I ease myself into my chair and out the back door, roll stealthily down the ramp. When I get to the sidewalk I check the windows to see if Avo or Ava are watching. All clear.

I'm free.

I head down to the bay to where the rowing club is. All by myself, without Loki grumping, "What do you want to do that for?" I switch between rolling along in the chair and staggering behind it, my bad leg dragging. A couple of runners pass, giving me curious stares. A lady with a fat border collie stops and asks, "Are you okay?" I say yes, thanks, trying not to gasp for breath. My palms sting.

I just make it to the grass beside the dock. The bay is calm, the tiniest breeze stirring the willows and rippling the reflections on the water. Half a dozen sculls are out already. I watch the coaches in aluminum runabouts buzzing around them, yelling. The coxswains blow their whistles. The rowers' shoulders gleam with sweat.

For a brilliant instant it's like I'm out there with them. I hear the water bubbling under the hull, feel the catch and pull of oars hooking the water. Feel my feet driving against the foot pedals, four pairs of arms moving like a single machine. I feel the absolute concentration as we stroke together, all in the same boat, pushing past the pain to win.

Right.

Slowly I come back to myself, a short, limpy girl hunched on the grass. It sinks in: no way ever again, not with these puny arms and the scarred aching butt I'm stuck with. I'm not the right shape to row. I'm not in the same boat with another person on the planet. I can't row. I don't even know if I can get home again.

I turn my chair around, both legs dragging now. It's all uphill now. Three blocks still to go, and my hands are scarlet and blistered. When I get out and walk, my hips scream with pain.

Lurching around the corner into James Street, I see a figure on the sidewalk. It's Avo. He strides jerkily toward me. Even from a distance he looks angry, his huge ears red. "Get in the chair," he shouts. I drop into it and he jerks it forward, bumps me over the cracks in the sidewalk.

Ava is at the front door. "Silly girl, silly girl!" She flaps her hands. "What are we supposed to think? That you run away again?"

"I didn't run away. I just went out by myself."

Avo wheels me around the side to the ramp and in the back door. Then he turns and heads out to the yard without another word. The screen slams behind him. "I'm sorry. I know I should have left a note," I call after him.

Ava bustles around the kitchen like a ruffled hen.

"You didn't really think I'd run away, did you?" I ask her. "I won't ever do that. You don't need to worry."

She pours me a glass of skim milk and puts muesli on the table. "Me, I don't think you run away. Not really. But your Avo, he worries."

If he worries, I guess he must care. "I went down to the water to watch the boats, Ava. It's a really nice place. Don't you ever go there?"

She shakes her head. "It is not so nice, I don't think. No place to walk."

"But there is. There's a nice paved path, with little trees and everything. They must have fixed it up since you were there. You should come down there with me to see it."

"Far for me to walk. I'm not so young anymore." She reaches

up for the framed picture that sits on the top shelf of the cabinet with the good china and glasses. I've already looked at it—it's ancient and faded. The girl has on a summer dress, white eyelet, I think it's called, pretty but not fancy, buttons down the front and a belt. She has dark curly hair and I wouldn't think she was even twenty. The guy is more solemn and he's wearing a suit, so he seems older.

Ava gazes at it for a moment and then hands it to me. "Then I was young like you. My wedding day."

"That's you and Avo?" I am amazed. I check out the boy's ears and they're big, although his hair mostly covers them, but not as big as Avo's ears now. I read somewhere that your ears go on growing until you die. "How old were you?"

"Seventeen." She's nestled into him and he has his arm around her tiny waist. They look like they can't believe how lucky they are. And here they are now, in this dark little house on a shabby street, all wrinkled and veiny and white-haired.

Does Ava ever look at this picture and think: Who took our bodies?

Chapter 14

Getting this excuse for a body back together is plenty to deal with right now. Can I ever in a million years turn it into anything like the one I had? I used to be tall with great muscle mass. Krystal's body is short and round. Big difference. Okay, I've dropped some pounds and maybe I'll even grow a bit. What else can I do but hope?

Plastic surgery could be an option down the line. One big problem is, I can't remember very clearly how I used to look. It's funny, I lived in my body for seventeen years but didn't really pay much attention to it. Are most people that vague about themselves, or am I just forgetting?

So my hair was blond, but how blond? How light did it bleach out in the sun? I remember I always had a few freckles in summer and my skin tended to burn, even with sunblock. My nose was straight, maybe a touch on the long side.

All those hours I spent staring in the mirror while I brushed my hair or put on mascara, and I can't say what made my eyes and lips any different from anybody else's. My eyes were blue and my mouth—well, it was just a mouth. I used to think my lower lip was too thin, but could I pick it out of a line-up?

I wouldn't know my ears if I tripped over them. Same with my knees, my ankles, my butt. I might recognize my shoulders—everybody always said I had rowers' shoulders, great definition. And I'd recognize my belly button, from the time I let Abby talk me into getting it pierced. When I rowed, the stud caught on my tank top and got infected. It left a little white scar, so I'd recognize that. Not much out of a whole heap of spare parts.

In Avo and Ava's bathroom there's a mirror I've been avoiding. When I blow-dry my hair, it's steamy enough that I don't have to look at my face. I've tried, and it makes me crazy. But I don't want to start school looking any worse than I have to.

Things Loki says make it sound like a bad place for getting picked on. To be honest, I'm scared. I always used to take friends for granted. People mostly liked me. Now I wonder if they will. Seems like there was something about Krystal that kids thought they could pick on and get away with. Well, they'll be in for a surprise if they try now. I may look like poor little Red Rose, but inside I'm still a tall white überbitch.

I square my shoulders and stare into the mirror. The face that stares back isn't a bad face, even if I hate it. Big dark eyes, long thick lashes. Skin's mostly cleared up now that I eat properly. But there is that unibrow and the incipient moustache on the upper lip. And the awful mop of long hair, brown at the roots, black at the ends, split like straw. It hangs over my shoulders, and I peer through the bangs like a pony. When I was Amy, I kept my hair just below my ears, wash and go. I need a haircut bad. Who can I ask to help me get one?

Ava? Joan? I decide Susan will be the lucky person—she said we could go shopping some time. When I get her on the phone, she's great. "Let me see how soon I can get an appointment," she says.

"It can't be too expensive. I've only got forty dollars saved."

"Don't you worry about that. My treat."

"But I need my eyebrows done too."

"They do that there. I'll fix it up." She calls back two minutes later to say that Renaldo, her stylist, can take me tomorrow.

I remember I've still got her favourite book that she lent me back in the hospital. I tell her I'll give it back.

"Did you like it?" she asks eagerly.

I don't want to tell her I forgot all about it. "I haven't quite finished it," I admit.

"Just keep it until you do."

She loves the book for some mysterious reason. It's about a sad girl with a nasty family who pick on her all the time. When she finds out she's got a bad heart and won't live more than a year, she really goes off the rails. She asks this wild guy to marry her and promises it'll only be for a year. That's as far as I got before I got distracted. I don't know why Susan is so keen for me to read it. There's nothing in it about switching bodies, as far as I can see.

I'm waiting on the front porch with my crutches next afternoon when she pulls up. She's amazed to see me out of the wheelchair. "You're sure you're not pushing the process too fast, Mia?" she frowns. "You shouldn't be putting too much strain on healing bones."

"It's okay. I'm being careful."

"But you have a powerful agenda."

I haven't been in Susan's car before, a fancy hybrid like my mother's. They're not cheap. I didn't know social workers got paid that well. "What does your husband do?" I ask. "If you don't mind me asking."

"He's a judge."

So I guess she can afford a haircut.

She's worrying about finding a parking place close enough to the hair salon, but there's one right outside. "I have good parking karma," I tell her. That's one thing that hasn't changed.

When we go in, Renaldo rushes over and makes a huge fuss over Susan. "What a surprise. I didn't see your name in the appointment book, darling."

"It's not for me. It's for Mia here."

He checks me out, lifts a piece of my hair like it's dirty Kleenex. "And what were we thinking of today?"

When I describe the haircut I used to have, he says, "I don't think that will work with your hair."

"She has some natural wave," Susan says encouragingly.

He sighs. "Let's give it a good conditioning and see what we have."

I lie back as someone named Elroy scrubs my head and rinses my hair. "Don't rub too hard," I tell him. "I was in an accident and a lot of it already fell out."

"Yeah?" He doesn't sound that interested. I lie back and enjoy the feel of a boy's fingers on my skull.

Renaldo is a little more positive as he combs my hair out. "You'll have to trust me," he says.

"He's very good," Susan reassures me.

"I'd also like to be blond," I say. Like I used to be. And maybe he could make me taller while he's at it.

"Forget *that*," Renaldo says firmly. "Blond would be awful with your colouring. Besides, it would cost a fortune to keep up. You'd have to have the roots done every two weeks."

Right—and who'd be paying for it? I can't expect Susan to.

"What about a few highlights?" she suggests.

After Renaldo puts in some foils, they shift me over to Lisa the cosmetologist. Soon as I see her eyebrows, little thin half-circles halfway up her forehead like an old silent-movie star, warning bells go off. "Just take out the hairs in the middle."

Lisa goes ahead and plucks what she wants and waxes a space above my nose. I've been looking down at my lap so as not to make eye contact in the mirror with that pudgy face. Now I'm watching Lisa like a hawk. I'm relieved to end up with two eyebrows like normal people, even though it hurts like hell.

"What about this?" I point to the dark fuzz on my upper lip. She waxes that off too, which *really* hurts. "You might want to think about laser down the road, hon," she says. "In the meantime, buy yourself some Nair."

All this must be costing Susan a fortune. "I'll pay you back," I promise her.

"I told you it's my treat."

"But I asked you to take me to get a haircut. I didn't mean for you to pay for everything."

"I don't have any daughters to fuss over, Mia. Just say thank you. Consider yourself a niece for a day."

After the foils come off, Renaldo does some cutting with a razor. It's not me I'm seeing in the mirror, more like a makeover on TV. Finally he whips the cape from my shoulders. "Ta-da!"

Susan's eyes catch mine in the mirror. "What a transformation!"

It is a million times better than it was, shoulder-length, straight, and glossy brown with amazing layers and glints of gold. I toss my head, and the layers float in slow motion. Some of the other stylists have come over. They're waiting for my reaction.

"Fantastic." I high-five Renaldo, corny as hell.

"So you like it?" Susan asks, once she's bundled me back in the car. "Because it's lovely, you know. It's amazing what a difference it makes."

It's a great haircut, very cool, and she paid for it. But if I'd gotten the cut I used to have, I would be one step closer to getting back to me. That's not how it's worked out. I don't look any more like Amy than I ever did.

"Not different enough," I murmur. Susan makes me repeat it. We haven't talked about my "problem" lately. I think she's hoping I'll forget.

"Let's leave that discussion until later, okay?" she says briskly. "Meanwhile, how's your energy holding up? Think you could handle a quick trip to the mall?"

I can be bought off pretty easy. At the Bay I pick up a dozen pairs of underpants, so I can throw out all of Krystal's thongs. Susan lets me get a couple of sports bras too, to squash down those big bouncy boobs I'm carrying around. They've subsided since I lost some flab, but they still feel way out of proportion.

The mall is packed with mothers outfitting daughters for going back to school. They must see me and Susan and think that's what we are too. A jab of anguish almost makes me double over. What's my real mother doing at this moment? Who is she getting ready to go back to school?

Chapter 15

On the first day of classes it's hot by eight o'clock. I'm dressed in my uniform, spotless cotton shirt buttoned to the neck and green and white school kilt, every pleat ironed sharp as a knife by Ava, knee socks and leg brace. I'm nervous.

"Don't worry." She pats me. "You look very nice. You will be fine."

"I'm not worrying." School is one thing I do well, or at least used to. All I care about is getting good marks and getting out: New plan, step 1. But I admit I'm kind of on edge. The handful of Goth kids we had at my old school got picked on. I don't care about making friends, I just don't want to make enemies. Because, oh God, it's going to be a long two years.

Ava hands me a plastic bag. "I make you a lunch, so you don't have to line up to buy."

"Thanks, Ava." Great. I'll look like a dork eating giant dill pickles and sardines.

Loki shows up like he said and pushes me to school in my chair. I carry my crutches jauntily over my shoulder. He doesn't say much, feeling glum about going back, I guess. "You scared?" he asks.

"Should I be?"

The vice-principal, Sister Mary Catharine, lets me park my

chair in the corner of the office waiting room. Loki or I can go get it any time. The school feels different than from when I was seeing the counsellor three weeks ago. It's packed, and the smell of teenage sweat is rising.

I hobble to my homeroom on crutches, and Loki leaves me there. I hobble into the room.

"Hey, Krystal, wow. Come sit over here," some girl says to me.

"Hey, Krystal, come sit on me," some boy calls out, and his friends snicker. I shoot them a glance of pure loathing and take a seat near the front. They shut up, maybe because the teacher is already there. His name is written on the board: MR. MCINTOSH. Glasses and spiky hair. When the bell goes, he takes attendance. He comes to "Mia Marques," and I say "here."

The guy ahead of me turns around and stares, and a couple of kids call out, "It's Krystal," like he's made a mistake.

"No, it's Mia," I say. "I changed it."

Somebody groans. Somebody else laughs. The teacher goes on with the roll.

"Hey, Krystal, how come you changed your name?" the girl in the row beside me asks.

I mutter, "I hate Krystal."

Half the class is plugged in, off in worlds of their own. Mr. McIntosh makes everyone put their music away. "No players, no phones, no texting. Any electronics turned on in class I confiscate and you'll have to collect them from the office." More groans.

Loki and I are in different homerooms but the same math class, which is second period, after English. When the teacher asks him a question, he says something stupid in a goofy way and everyone laughs. He's not stupid. Why is he acting like he is? When I give the right answer, everybody turns around and stares again. I guess Krystal wouldn't have put her hand up. But why shouldn't I?

A couple of people in the hall say hi and ask what happened to me, but I just say hi back and head for the washroom. I'm not up for conversation. One girl lets the washroom door slam in my face, but then another comes along and holds it open. "What did you do to your leg?" she asks.

I give her the official line. "Got hit by a truck."

"Wow."

At lunchtime Loki brings my chair and I drop into it. My shoulders and my back ache, and my armpits are raw from the crutches. When Loki goes up to buy his lunch, he leaves me on my own near the back of the cafeteria. I'm feeling kind of exposed and tense.

"This must be the cripps corner."

I whip around to snarl. A guy and a girl are standing there. He's on crutches, a cast halfway up his leg. "Okay if we sit down?" He nods at the empty places beside me.

His girlfriend helps him get settled, his leg stuck out from the table. "So what happened to you?" he asks.

"I got hit by a truck."

"Cool. I got mine water-skiing. Snapped my tibia." He launches into the story.

Then Loki is back, and all around me people are chowing down on pizza and fries. I get out Ava's grocery bag and reach cautiously inside. Yogourt, carrot and celery sticks, grapes. Chicken on rye. I'm so grateful my eyes swim.

We're still eating when Brittany and Real Blond come over. Or maybe it's not Real Blond from the hospital, because this one's skirt is a bit longer.

"You owe me six bucks for that call on my sister's cell," Brittany says, hands on her hips.

I dig in my pencil case. "All I've got on me is a five. I'll give you a loonie tomorrow."

She takes it, frowning at it in surprise. "Okay, but don't forget."

"Don't go spending it," Loki tells her. "That's your sister's money, not yours."

"If she's lucky," says Brittany, gazing at me. "You look different," she says finally.

"Yeah, duh, she was in an accident," says Waterski Boy. "She almost died." Us cripps stick together.

"No, I mean—" She stares at me appraisingly. "Uh, different better. Hair and stuff."

"Maybe she got switched at the hospital," Real Blond says. "You know, like with babies, sometimes they get them mixed up and the parents come home with the wrong ones and nobody knows?"

Everybody laughs, including me. She's way closer to the truth than she knows.

Waterski Boy's girlfriend says, "There's this old kids' book I read, about two sisters marooned on a desert island, with all these babies."

"*Baby Island*," says Real Blond.

"Yeah, that's it. And two of the babies are identical twins and the only way even their own mother can tell them apart is how they're dressed. And the girls take the babies' clothes off to bathe them and then they're terrified they've mixed them up, because nobody'll never ever be able to tell which is which."

Close again. Anyway, already I've got a clique and we're talking about books and identity switches. And I thought they might turn on me like sharks smelling blood.

On the way home the Real Blond girl comes up and walks along with me and Loki. "I know you live near me," she says. "I've seen you."

I realize now where I've seen her before—not with Brittany but with her little sister, walking a dog. Her name's actually Shelley. She says she has a brother as well—a real, normal family. "What happened to you, you know, after the accident?" she asks. Turns out she was on the same drama-class trip that day. "It was awful scary. Nobody knew if you were going to live."

I give her the standard version. She asks questions like she's actually interested. When we get to my house, she says, "See you guys later, okay?"

"Friggin' weird," says Loki, looking at her over his shoulder. "She never talked to us before."

Back home I wheel myself straight to my room and lie down. I am totally wiped from being on crutches for so long. Ten seconds later Ava is outside in the hall. "How was the school?" she asks. She cracks open the door.

I prop myself on my elbow and manage a smile. "Not as bad as I thought. Loki helped me a lot. I might even have some friends." All in all, it could have been worse. Just twenty-one months and twenty-odd days to go.

Her face lights up with relief.

"And thanks for the great lunch, Ava."

Susan phones later to see how I got on. "Did they like your hair?"

And I say, yeah, Brittany did. The hair was the right thing to do.

By the end of the week I decide that, except for being Catholic, Regi is really not that much different from my old school. I was afraid it might be tough, with all those young dudes with pit bulls I've seen on the street. I thought everybody'd be doing drug deals in the hall and carrying weapons, but they're just ordinary kids. The teachers are generally okay too. The one that teaches English is young and a bit spaced out. She lets the class get away with too much, but we had plenty of those at my old school too.

The one part I find strange is all the prayers. In my old school, if you even mentioned God without giving equal time to Mohammed and Buddha and Gitchi Manitou, you'd be up on a human rights charge. I don't know much about Catholicism, but when they start talking about loaves and fishes and virgin birth and the Father, Son and Holy Ghost, I listen. It's all fantastical, magic stuff, and nobody's saying, "Oh, that could not happen." And it's way weirder than what's happened to me. I mean, Jesus walks on water and he stops a storm. He even brings a dead guy back to life. Is it just because it happened in the old days, they think nothing like that happens now? Maybe if I got up on the stage at assembly and told my story, they'd make me a saint.

Burn me at the stake, more likely.

Chapter 16

Sometimes I wake up in the night and go crazy wondering what she's doing, the girl in my body, and how I'm going to find out. If it really is Krystal, how on earth can she cope? What kind of awful mess is she making of my life?

My heart starts pounding and I have to hold myself back from crawling out of bed to the phone. What stops me is my fear of getting Avo mad at me and sending me away. I talk myself down: *You have to wait until you get stronger.* Right now it takes all the strength I've got just to get out of bed.

A few weeks into September Loki turns up with a black eye and a cut, swollen lip.

"Wow. What happened?" I ask. "Fall off your skateboard?"

"Naw," he mutters. "Fight with my brother."

His hair half covers the eye but when I look close, it's a real mess, purple and swollen shut. "Did you go to emergency?"

"What for?"

"Because you're hurt!"

"I got beat up, that's all. What are they gonna do?"

At lunchtime Waterski Boy sees him and whistles. "Trying to get into the cripps club, eh? Good one." Everybody laughs. Brittany and Shelley tease him about his shiner. Loki grins, his face lopsided. He likes the attention.

I don't think it's funny. From the way he moves, he's hurting. His hands are nicked and bruised. I can imagine the rest of him is pretty bad too. By the end of the day he's like some kind of one-eyed monster. "Are your ribs okay?" I ask on the way home. He's sort of wheezing.

"Yeah, sure."

"Did your brother really do all that to you?"

"Yeah, he's a head case. Thinks he's some kind of kick-boxer."

I can't imagine anyone in my family inflicting this kind of damage and me being so cool about it. "What did your mother say?"

"She's pissed at him."

"Pissed! She should be throwing him out!"

"Get real." I can't see his face, because he's pushing me in the chair, but he sounds angry. "You don't know anything, do you?"

I turn in my chair. He glares back at me from his one good eye. He looks terrible. It's true, I don't know anything, especially not about him. I've never been to his house, and I don't want to. He talks all the time about his mother and brother and his brother's tough friends, but I've never got the sense he was afraid or anything. What kind of brother does this to you?

I wonder if he's lying. I wonder if maybe his father did it, or his mother's boyfriend. "I heard you got called out of class to go to the guidance office. What did the counsellor say about it?"

"Nothing. I didn't tell her nothing."

"So who really did that to you, Loki? What really happened?"

"Shut up. I told you." He gives the chair a shove and my head snaps back.

"Hey, easy!"

Then he asks, "What happened to Krystal?"

"Krystal? What do you mean, *Krystal*?" I twist around again in the chair in amazement.

He's glowering. "If you were Krystal, you'd know my life is shit. So if you're not her, what happened to her?" The chair lurches over a pothole and I nearly fall out on my head.

"Watch it, would you!" I yell. "I told you, she's in my body, as far as I know. What's the matter with you? Why are you getting mad at me? I told you I wasn't her, right from the start."

He starts to say something, then stops, his mouth working. "Where is she?" he asks finally.

"Toronto, I guess. That's why you brought me Brittany's sister's cellphone, remember? So I could call her."

"Did you get her?"

"No. You wouldn't get the phone for me again. The only person I talked to was my mother. She said she—Krystal, you know—was in bad shape."

I told him all along I wasn't Krystal. I told him we got switched. He's never believed me until now, but that's not my fault. He's the one who says I have amnesia.

He pushes me to my back door and walks away without a word. I don't know why he's so angry with me. I'm not the one who's just worked him over. I've never done anything to him—in fact, I've treated him better than a lot of his no-neck skater friends. And I don't fall for that line of his that he's stupid.

I know he thinks I'm a bitch and a stuck-up snob, and maybe he's right. But what am I going to do if he doesn't like me anymore and refuses to help me? I won't be able to manage.

Avo is in his garden, cleaning up the tomato beds. He catches my eye. "Not very happy," he says. I don't know if he means me or Loki.

"Poor boy." So he means Loki. I watch him work for a while, carting away dead leaves, digging in compost. Slowly my heart stops hammering. Then I go in and change into my jeans and tell

Ava I'm going down to watch the rowers. I've been down a couple of times on my own. They don't try to stop me anymore, just want me to let them know where I am.

I use my method of pushing the chair and, when I get tired, sitting in it and rolling myself along. I still lurch when I walk, and one leg drags. People give me funny looks and sometimes ask if I need help. Ava says I'm walking better, but I'm not sure it's true. The physio isn't promising I'll ever walk without a limp.

Down at the bay I sit on the grass and brood. I'm still feeling shaken about what happened with Loki. I can't get the look on his face out of my mind, like I'm some kind of alien. And he *knows* me. Imagine how other people will react.

I'm still brooding when the doors to the boatsheds open and people come out, carrying a couple of shells to the dock. A minute or two later they're gliding across the water, their wakes fanning out in criss-crossing Vs. They look so serene and powerful, perfectly in tune. With all my heart I wish I was out there with them.

A shadow falls across the grass. I look up and see this tall, skinny guy, late thirties maybe. "I've seen you here before," he says. I've seen him around the boatsheds too. "Mind if I sit down?"

I say no, and he puts out his hand, which I shake. "Mike Flynn. I coach with the club."

"I'm Mia."

"You seem pretty interested in the rowing, Mia."

"I used to row."

"Oh, yeah?" He looks at me curiously. "I wouldn't have pegged you for a rower."

"For my old school in Toronto, Lawrence Park. I know I don't look like a rower now. I was in an accident. I'm shorter than before it happened." Not a lie.

"You must have been really banged up. Car accident?"

"Sort of. I was in the hospital from the May 24 weekend until August."

"That's a long time. So you've moved here recently? Where do you go to school?"

"Regi."

"Regi has a good rowing team. Are you thinking about joining? That is, uh—"

"I don't know if I'll be able to row again."

He hits his forehead with his hand. "Tactless question. I knew the minute the words were out of my mouth. Sorry." He waves to a couple of girls heading in to the clubhouse and calls them over. "Do you know Helen and Tracy? They're on the Regi team."

They're obviously rowers, rangy and broad-shouldered. Like I used to be. I shake my head. "I just started at Regi this fall. I hardly know anybody."

He introduces us. One of them—Tracy—stares at me. "Aren't you—that girl—didn't you—"

I have an awful feeling she's going to say Krystal. "I'm Mia," I say quickly. "I just moved here from Toronto. I rowed on my school's junior team."

"Branksome?" Helen's eyes narrow.

"No, Lawrence Park."

They both nod. Not the dreaded Branksome, or the dreaded Havergal. I talk about Lawrence Park rowing against Kingston at the Henley regatta in St. Catharine's in August. I know this because I googled the results in the school library. Lawrence Park didn't do as well as the year before. My friends Elly and Jenn won the under-twenty-three women's pair on the two-thousand-metre course, but they lost to Victoria in the senior women's four.

I watch the puzzled frown leave Tracy's face. I seem to have convinced her she's got me mixed up with someone else. They all talk about Cataraqui's record this year, and then head off to the dock. I'm forgotten.

But on the way home I break out in goosebumps over what I've done. "You're the girl—" Tracy said. I saw it in her eyes—the girl who was in the accident and in a coma. I've got to be famous for that. And who knows what else?

All she has to do is say around school, "Remember that no-hoper Goth girl who walked into a truck in Toronto? She's changed her name and started impersonating somebody who's supposed to be a hotshot rower." I'll be dead.

But then I think, Regi's a big school, more than fifteen hundred kids. Maybe I won't run into her again and she'll forget about it. But that means I can't go down and watch the rowing anymore either, and that idea just about kills me.

Chapter 17

For a whole week Loki avoids me, never mind that he's the best and really only friend I have in this life. Avo takes me to school and Real Blond Shelley, the one with the nice family who lives near me, takes me home. But mostly I have to get around all day on my own, which is no picnic. I can't blame Loki. This thing that's happened to me makes me crazy, so it probably doesn't make him feel very sane either.

One day he comes up to me in the hall. He gets right to the point. "Did you call her yet?"

"From where? The public telephone outside the school office?"

"Your grandparents got a phone."

I don't want to do that. After I got out of the hospital Susan gave me a big talk about how I shouldn't try calling. How I had to live inside the body I was in. Not that I think she'd check up on me with Ava. On the other hand, she might.

"Your mother's got a phone," I snap back. "I'll give you the number. *You* call."

After that he'll talk to me if I speak first, but he makes it clear he doesn't want to spend much time with me. We still see each other every day at school, but he sits with his skater friends at lunch now. Those big-pants morons don't have much use for me. They're not like some guys at school who actually think a chick on crutches is sexy—no thanks. And a couple of creeps who obviously knew Krystal in ways I don't like to think about. Or maybe that's not fair to her. Maybe they just wanted to, figured they could if they tried.

If I ask Loki for help with something, he'll do it, usually. I call him about math homework, but it's not like before, when I was in the hospital. He's way spikier. If I push him too hard, he asks, "Why do you keep calling me?"

"I don't know why I call you. You are such a jerk."

After I hang up, I know the real answer: I miss him. Which is funny, since I used to think he was kind of dumb. I still sort of do, but then I've always secretly thought I was smarter than everybody else. I used to make fun of Loki for having to tell me the whole plot of every movie he ever saw, but I liked it too, the way he got so excited about all the stories. He's not dumb, though.

Anyway, actually, I do have friends besides Loki. Waterski Boy and his girlfriend, for example. Their real names are Andrew and Jessica, and they're nice to hang around with. Even though Andrew isn't a cripp anymore, he still puts on a big limp when he sees me. Brittany's gone off with some guy she mouth-mashes in the halls, but Shelley is more my friend now than hers.

A couple of times Shelley and I have gone down together to watch the rowers. Her dog Sunny and little sister Cayley come too. Cayley loves my wheelchair and even though I don't really need it much now, she wants to take it. She pushes me, and sometimes she or Shelley takes a turn and I push. Ava and Avo like it that I'm friends with them. Their mother's Portuguese too, and Avo gives them some of his tomatoes to take home.

I also have Susan to talk to if I need to, and Krystal's foster mom Joan drops around sometimes. And I've got Ava and Avo. Not that I do much with them, but we're getting on okay. Avo leaves a little blue bowl of cherry tomatoes, not quite ripe, on the table for me at breakfast. "Avo picked these for you," Ava says. "The way you like them." He noticed! Sometimes instead of tomatoes I find a few late raspberries glowing in the tiny bowl. And Ava helped me paint my room—orange-melon. It sounds terrible, but it came out great. Sometimes we go grocery shopping together at No Frills. Loki calls it No Thrills.

One day I'm at the supermarket by myself, getting milk for Ava, when I see phone cards by the cash. Why didn't I think of it before? I can make long distance calls and not leave a trace on Ava and Avo's phone. And if you call on a card, it only shows up on the caller ID at the other end as a number.

I buy a ten-dollar card. Next time I'm alone in the house, I use it. I can look out the kitchen window and keep my eye on Avo working in the garden. If he starts to come in, I'll hang up the phone.

I punch in our home number, my palms going damp, and get a message: my mom's voice. "*We can't answer right now . . . Leave us a message.*"

Who's us? Mom and *her*?

Just then Avo stomps toward the ramp. I quickly hang up and slip into my room, closing the door. I sit on the bed with Mom's voice still echoing in my head, every cell in my body buzzing.

I'm upset, sure. But not as much as I could be. Not like that time in the hospital when I went nuts. And as I sit there I realize I've been so busy lately that I haven't been missing Mom so much as at first. Like when someone dies, the more time passes, the further away the feelings get. The missing isn't so painful. But it's really sad that the person gets further and further away.

I still remember clear as anything how nice Mom smells and what great hair she has—like Teflon, no amount of wind can wreck it. And how she'll take me shopping whenever I ask. When I actually think about it, we never did a lot else together. It was

Dad's job to take me skiing, take me to Gran's, and to Grandma and Grandpa's, take me to the Calgary Stampede. Mom was busy getting her career off the ground.

Ava and Avo and me, we always eat supper together. With Mom it was a sticky note on the fridge: "Frozen lasagna in the freezer!" After she and Dad broke up, I know it was hard for her to be there for me. But that was more or less okay. I didn't want to think about them breaking up. I had my friends. And rowing. And I had Wolfie. I wonder if he still thinks about me.

I had cable hookup, my laptop, great clothes, CDs and DVDs. And the Muskoka cottage. I never realized how privileged I was. I mean, I knew I was privileged, but compared to lots of other girls I knew, no big deal. I didn't have any more than what everybody on television has. No more than I deserved, right?

I knew nothing. Now I've seen what a raw deal lots of other people like Krystal get. And it's not their fault. Not their choice. People don't get to choose what body they're put into. Like, people get born into bodies in the middle of a genocide war in Darfur, and they don't get to worry about how tall they are or whether they'll ever be able to row. They're too busy worrying about how they're going to stay alive for another day.

I keep thinking that maybe this has happened because I'm supposed to understand what it's like to be in someone else's shoes, and when I get it, I'll be allowed to go back to my cushy life. So, okay, I get it. Can I go back now?

Nothing happens.

Susan calls. "It's getting cooler," she says. "You're going to need some warmer clothes." On the way to the mall, she tells me I'm looking steadier on my feet than the last time we got together. She talks about how the insurance case is going. "The trucking firm is dragging it out. The longer they can hold off, the better shape they hope you'll be in, and the less they'll have to pay."

"How do they know how I'm doing? Nobody's been to see me that I know of." Are there spies lurking in the halls at Regi?

"The company is in touch with the hospital. Our lawyer is telling them you need the money now to fully recover. They've offered to settle for one hundred thousand dollars."

"Wow! Take it!"

"It sounds like a lot of money, but it isn't really."

"Isn't it a lot more than you thought we could get?"

"You'll have other medical expenses that will need to be covered. And who knows what kind of long-term damage may show up down the road?" She glances over at me, apologetic. "Sorry, Mia, that's not a nice thing to think about, but we need to be hard-nosed. It's your future."

She's right. It'll take millions to get this crappy body into the shape I want.

"I'm thinking about breast reduction," I tell her.

"What? Why? You have beautiful breasts!"

"I hate them. It's like having a couple of turnips tied around my neck."

"They're not *that* big, Mia."

"Because I wear a sports bra all the time. Guys still stare at them. They get in my way."

"Lots of women would pay to have breasts like yours."

"I'll sell, if you know anybody who's buying."

"I don't think that's how it works."

When we make a quick stop at a Shopper's Drug Mart so Susan can pick up a prescription, I wait in the car. She takes her wallet and leaves me with her bag—the big floppy leather one that gapes open. It's like a bomb's gone off inside, all her glasses cases and datebooks and crap. Then I see her cellphone. I don't think about it. I grab it and punch in my number.

And get myself.

It's Amy. I'm not answering. Leave me a message, okay?

I nearly drop the phone. It's still my old message! Nobody's changed it. But that's good—or at least I think it is. If she'd snuffed it, wouldn't they have closed her account?

But I can't leave a message, even if I wanted to, because the message box is full. "Goddammit, girl," I mutter, "clear your messages."

Then I remember—*I'm* Amy, they're *my* messages. I punch in my password. And there they all are, my friends.

Elly. "Amy, if you can hear this, babe, I love you."

Damian. "Ame, I'm missing you something awful. I'm praying for you."

Melissa Hunt. "Amy, everybody on the team sends their love. Jan Pringle has taken your place, but we're not the same team anymore. Hurry back."

Gabby says my name and starts crying. Then, then, Nate comes on. "Amy," he says, his voice husky. He clears his throat. "Amy, I just wanted to hear your voice. I'm really sorry about what happened. I wish I could have—I wish—"

Brief silence. "I'd give anything for you to get better."

I replay them all. When I get to Nate again, I imagine him standing at the window of his parents' house, gazing out at the back deck with the phone in his hand. His shoulders are hunched in that way that makes me want to put a hand between his shoulder blades and say, "Let go." I take every bit of feeling I can get from his "I wish."

Susan opens the car door and slides in. "Sorry to take so long." Then she sees my face.

I switch her phone off and put it back in her bag. "I used your cell to make a call." I wipe my eyes with the back of my hand.

Her lips go tight. "I trusted you, Mia."

"What's not to trust? I'm telling you, aren't I? I'm not lying about it."

"Only because I caught you in the act."

"I would have told you. It would have shown up as the last number dialed anyway, for godsakes! Besides, I never promised you I wouldn't."

She turns the key in the ignition, puts the car in gear, checks the rear view mirror as she backs out. Pulls out onto the road. It must be five minutes before she says anything.

"Did you get through?" she asks.

Chapter 18

October. Avo listens to the weather all the time on the radio, worrying about frost. If there's a chance of it, he covers all his plants with sheets. The kitchen counter is crowded with the bottles of tomatoes Ava boils in a big pot on the stove. Avo sits at the table squashing seeds onto paper towels, and when I ask him why, he says. "For next year."

"Why don't you just buy seeds?" I ask.

He gives me a look like I should smarten up. "These are better." Which is true.

If I was rowing, I'd be training every day. Not so much on the river, not until spring, but running or weights or working on the machines. I can't do that, but I've joined the yoga club at school. Yoga's great for flexibility, and it's gentle, right? It drives me nuts that I can't do the poses like I used to when I was Amy. I can't squat because of my scar tissue. My legs are too short and my hamstrings are too tight. My arms won't reach where they're supposed to. My balance is off—I try to stand on one leg and keel over. Everything hurts, and the pain makes me stream with sweat.

"Don't forget to breathe," Ms. Kemp says, looking right at me. I forget all the time. After the first session, she takes me aside and asks if I should be doing yoga so soon after my accident.

"You mean, I'm not good enough to be in the club?" Okay, so I'm on crutches—people with disabilities have rights too.

"No, no, I don't mean that. I mean you need to take it a little easier. This is yoga, not a triathlon. You're going at it like your life depends on it."

Maybe not my life, but my future. But okay, I get it.

It's a couple of weeks before I have the overwhelming urge to call home again. Avo and Ava are out somewhere and I've still got nine dollars and sixty-seven cents left on my card.

This time I get a real person, a guy. He sounds vaguely familiar, but he sure isn't Dad.

I swallow hard. "Can I speak to Amy?" My voice sounds high and childish.

"You don't have her cell number?"

"Oh—is it the same as it was? I moved away from Toronto," I ad lib. "I just heard that she was in an accident."

"That's right, the poor kid. She had us all pretty scared for a while. She's doing better now."

"Is she at school?"

"No, actually, she hasn't been able to manage it. Next semester she'll go back."

He thinks her cell number is still the same, so I hang up and call it. I get her message—the same one, my old voice. She can't be doing all that well if she hasn't even changed my message.

After that I call her every time I'm in the house by myself, until the card runs out. Still no answer, but I listen to the messages. There aren't any new ones, but I play the old ones I've saved over and over.

Amy, if you can hear this, babe, I love you . . . Ame, I'm missing you something awful. I'm praying for you . . . Everybody sends their love. We're not the same team without you. Hurry back.

And then Nate. It's all I've got of him now. I play it over and over, listening for something in his voice I might have missed. He sounds so sad.

Amy, uh, Amy, I'm really sorry for what happened. Good luck.

I'm longing for Toronto. I know nothing will ever be the same, but I'd still give both my crutches just to be there. Actually, I'd give those away for a lot less. I just want to sit in some little café and watch people going by. Susan goes to Toronto quite a lot with her job, I know—she has meetings there. I start nagging her to take me with her. "I know my way around. You could just drop me somewhere and pick me up at the end of the day."

She gets all stiff around the mouth. "I wouldn't feel comfortable doing that."

"Why not? What do you think I'll do, become a suicide bomber? Go around to my house and blow her up? I won't. I just miss Toronto."

"It could be disastrous for you."

"I don't have to go with you. I could just go on my own," I point out. "Take the train or the bus."

"You could. I hope you won't, though. Your grandparents would never agree to it. You're doing so well, Mia. Concentrate on getting better. On building strength."

"I'll be going to U of T," I remind her. "I'm aiming for a scholarship."

"Good for you. But that's a year and a half away, and things will feel different by then. And I think you should consider staying here for university, Mia. Don't underestimate what you'll still be coping with. You're still at risk. You have support here. Your grandparents, your friends."

"What do you mean, at risk? What am I coping with?"

I'm putting her on the spot. She doesn't like to talk about the body switch. But I really want to know why she thinks it's so dangerous for me. This time she meets my eyes. "If your reality is at odds with that of everyone around you, it's a terrible strain to live under."

My reality. It's not like I can join some support group for it. Is there even a word for it? I've googled "body switching." Some really weird stuff comes up. Reincarnation is as close as I can get. "You mean if everybody else thinks this can't happen, even though I know it has, it could make me crazy?"

"Having a different reality from the rest of your community is a pretty good definition of insanity already, Mia."

"But my reality is the truth!" It's a good thing we're in the car with the windows up, because all of a sudden I'm shouting. "You know it's the truth. Why should I try to live like it's not? Isn't truth supposed to set you free?"

She sighs. "You know what happens to people who tell truths that no one else can believe?"

Yeah, I know.

There's a professional development day coming up in a week or two, meaning we'll get the day off school. I won't have anything to do except study—what a loser. I'll just hang around the house, maybe go over to Shelley's later and watch a movie. In Toronto I used to love PD days, sleeping in late, hanging out with my friends, going downtown to buy something funky.

Suddenly I know what I'm going to do with my PD day.

I find out there's a bus leaving at eight fifteen every morning. I can be in Toronto by eleven. I have enough allowance saved to cover a day-return ticket, food, and the subway fares. I can spend the whole day there and get a bus back at three and be home for supper. I won't even have to tell Ava and Avo. They don't have to know it's a PD day. They won't know the difference. I'll just get up like I'm going to school and call a cab from Tim Hortons to take me to the bus.

I plan every detail out so there'll be no slip-ups. I won't take my crutches or my cane: people notice. I need to be inconspicuous. I won't be able to carry much because I'll get tired. I'll take music, money, my travelling mug, dark glasses, and a book I have to read for English. Hope it doesn't rain, because an umbrella is too heavy. The long-range forecast says cloudy, not too cold for the first day of November. A 10 percent possibility of rain, but that's not bad.

What am I going to do when I get there? I could do some early Christmas shopping, get something cool for Loki, because it'll be only seven weeks to Christmas. I could drop in at the rowing club, except there won't be much going on. I'll go by Latifa's, my gang's old hangout. Maybe it'll be a PD day in Toronto too. Maybe I'll even see somebody I know. Just the thought is enough to make my palms sweat, so I don't even let myself think about why I'm really going.

My mind goes there anyway. Of course I'm going to Toronto to go home. I won't do anything stupid. I don't plan to knock on the door and say, "Hey, everybody, it's me, I'm back!" I guess I could pretend I wanted to drop some stuff off for Amy, or say I was selling Girl Guide cookies. I'll think of something—something that won't get me arrested for trespassing—when I get there.

Chapter 19

My alarm goes off at five thirty. I dress in my good jeans and a jacket, a navy wool scarf. I had my hair cut last week, went on my own this time, couldn't afford streaks but I look pretty good. Normal for the neighbourhood I used to live in. I leave a note on the kitchen table for Ava, on one of the cardboard ovals she saves out of Kleenex boxes for her lists: *I've got things to do, probably won't get home until late, after five. See you then.* She's made me a sandwich, so I get it out of the fridge, and a yogourt, and put them in my pack. I take a banana out of the fruit bowl.

Everything goes smoothly and I'm at the bus station with twenty minutes to spare. I buy a coffee and a muffin. The bus isn't crowded, just some sleepy people who started out in Montreal, and half a dozen of us getting on here. I find a seat by myself halfway to the back. Just before the driver shuts the door, some guy comes running up. He's pretty pleased he's made it, I can see. He stops next to me in the aisle and makes like he's going to sit down. He can't though, because I've got my backpack on the empty seat. "Plenty more seats back there," I say before he can open his mouth.

The last thing I want is some goofy kid talking my ear off all the way to Toronto. Anyway, I'm tired. I didn't sleep much. I plug myself into my music and gaze out the window.

I hardly see the scenery going past. It's brown and lifeless anyway. All I'm thinking about now is Toronto. I wonder what Mom's doing at this moment. Coming out of the shower, probably, blow-drying her hair. I think about our eyes meeting when she opens the front door, and what I'll say. "I've come to see Amy"—what if she says no? I'm so wired I can't eat my muffin. I feel sick.

All that changes when we get to the station. I come out the Dundas Street exit and get a lungful of city that just about knocks me off my feet. Car exhaust, cigarette smoke, pigeon shit, who knows what it is? I don't mean it smells bad, just Essence of Toronto. I'm sore from sitting on the bus, limping pretty badly, but I don't care. I know I should be saving my strength but I want to cover ground, fill my head up with the place. I walk down Bay Street along the edge of Chinatown, past City Hall. It's all so *real*. People look different from Kingston people. It's hard to say how— like it's a parallel universe.

Queen Street isn't far, so I hike over to a crepe place I know and order a caramel latte. It is so fantastic to be sitting somewhere so cool but everybody thinks it's normal. My hip and leg hurt, though. It's going to be harder getting around than I thought. I should have saved my energy for getting to the one place I really want to go.

I pour the rest of my latte into my own mug and hurry to catch a streetcar to the subway. At Davisville I get out and head for home. I'm tingling now with how familiar everything is. I feel like a secret agent, but scared out of my mind too. The Yonge Street shops are already decorated for Christmas, but tastefully, of course, with tiny white lights and green velvet bows. It's four blocks to our house but they're long ones. At least the sun has come out. Twittering sparrows explode out of a hedge as I walk past. I'm quivering, thinking that I could run into anybody. And

I do see someone I recognize, a woman with a shopping cart. I don't know her name or anything, but she always wears sensible shoes and a beret even in summer. I want to throw my arms around her, but I just say hi. She nods, probably wondering why some strange girl is speaking to her.

Our house is two doors down from the primary school. Across from the schoolyard there's a park. I sit on a bench in a sunny spot and stare at my house. My heart is thudding.

The house is so big, red brick and shingle, with the same round evergreens in front. I don't know if those trees grow that way or somebody has to cut them. I never paid any attention to things like that. Nothing's changed. I can see the window of my old room on the third floor, but no signs of life. Wolfie must be home, even if nobody else is.

I feel such a rush of longing for my old life. Every cell in my body is buzzing so loudly my ears ring. How weird is this? I must be the only person in the world sitting and waiting for herself to come out the front door.

But nobody notices anything odd: All they see is a girl in dark glasses drinking coffee on a bench. My disguise is complete. Mothers go by me pushing strollers, a grey-haired man heads past with a black-eyed baby in a carrier. The dog-walkers stand around and talk while their dogs sniff each other. The walkers don't seem to care how they look holding plastic bags of warm dog poo.

A bell rings at the school. Late recess or early lunch? The playground fills with little kids. I didn't go to that school, because we only moved here when I was in grade seven. Memories start to flood in of walking up and down this park about a million times with Wolfie and my own plastic bag, and wishing he'd hurry up. Of putting up Christmas lights with Dad and my sister, and all of us getting mad at each other when it didn't go right. I let myself wonder how my sister and her baby, little Stacey, are doing. I hardly think of them anymore now—it makes me feel bad. Stacey might be walking now, even talking. I never even saw her crawling.

Still no signs of life at our house. Our garage is behind, on a back lane that starts at the corner. From where I'm sitting, I can see if any cars leave or turn into the lane. I'm getting stiff, and my head aches from staring behind my dark glasses, back and forth from the front door of the house to the corner. Sooner or later someone is going to notice how long I've been here. I get up and stroll to the end of the street. I want to walk down the lane to see if there are any cars in our driveway, but I'm afraid I'll miss someone leaving by the front door.

Finally I do go down the lane, but I don't see any cars. They could be in the garage, but there's no window. I try to peer through the fence into the backyard, because maybe Wolfie is there, but there isn't a crack. I call his name—no answering bark.

I sit for another half hour on the bench in the park and eat my banana. Time's passing and I'm getting desperate. I have to do something.

Just then a silver hybrid whips down the road and turns into our lane, so fast I nearly miss it. I catch a flash of sleek blond hair and sunglasses. Mom!

And I'm on my feet, racing after her. I don't think about what I'll say. There's not a thought in my head but running, running to my mother. When I round the corner I see the car in the drive. It's such a long block and I'm not flying any more, my feathers are clipped. I'm hobbling and gasping.

I'm almost there when Mom strides back out the gate from the house. She must have forgotten something, she must have come back home to get it—she's always doing that, rushing around forgetting things. She's left the engine going, and when she flings open the car door, a blast of CBC rushes out. She doesn't even see me, just hops in and slams the door and backs into the street again. She almost runs me down.

Then she does see me, standing on the sidewalk.

"*Mom!*" I scream and frantically wave.

She's in the middle of putting on her sunglasses. She flashes me a brilliant smile and waves back. And drives away.

"Mom! Mom, wait!" I run and call after her until she turns the corner.

The street is empty. Very empty. I sag against the fence. My mother saw me but she didn't know me. She didn't hear me call.

I sit down on the curb. I don't know how long I've been crying when an elderly man walks past. He's not anyone I know. He hesitates, then doubles back. "Are you hurt, young lady?" He has an English accent. "Come now, it can't be as bad as all that."

I pull a crumpled Kleenex from my pocket and wipe my eyes and blow my nose. "I'm all right."

The sun glints on his glasses. "Well, then. That's better." He touches the brim of his hat and walks quickly on.

I'm not really all right. What does he know about how bad it can be? How could it be worse? My mom almost ran over me! And that's nothing compared to what's wrong with my life.

I unlatch the back gate and stumble down the path. I climb the backdoor steps and knock hard at the door. If Krystal's in there, I'll make her talk to me. She can't hide forever.

A dog barks upstairs—Wolfie! Lying on somebody's bed, I bet. I knock harder.

The barking descends the stairs. Now it's on the other side of the door. I turn the handle but it's locked. "Wolfie, it's me," I call to him.

He goes absolutely nuts. I press my cheek against the door. "You silly old thing," I croon. "It's okay. You don't understand why I don't open the door, do you? I would if I could, darling." I keep on talking until he finally stops barking. I slide down until I'm sitting on the steps. And there we are, me on one side, my dog on the other.

He woofs, like he's trying to talk to me. He whines. Nobody

else comes. We talk about how it used to be. For a long time.

Suddenly I look at my watch. It's two thirty! My bus! I scramble to my feet, pull on my pack.

Then I put my cheek against the door again. "Bye, darling," I say. "Don't worry, I'll be back. I promise." I can still hear him howling when I turn the corner. It breaks my heart.

Chapter 20

The way to the subway feels a lot longer now. One train pulls out just as I get to the platform, and the next one takes ages to come. When it does, it's packed with kids on their way home from school. They're all talking and joking around, not a care in the world except maybe homework. Of course nobody thinks of giving me a seat, and the pain in my legs is like fire.

When I get to the station, the three o'clock bus has left. There won't be another one for an hour. I don't have enough money to take the train instead—in fact, all I have left is a bunch of change. Why did I spend so much on food at that stupid place on Queen Street! I've got to call Ava, make some excuse for being late. I don't want to lie to her, but it's an emergency. I'll tell her I'm still at school, or over at Shelley's. I'll think of something.

I've never made a long-distance call from a pay phone. It can't be that hard—people do manage it, people who can't afford cellphones. When the lady in line ahead of me hangs up, I ask her how it works. "Dial zero for the operator," she says. I guess I could have figured that out.

"I want to make a call to Kingston," I tell the operator.

"That will be three dollars for five minutes," she says. I give her the number and she tells me, "Deposit the coins now." I put in everything I have except pennies.

"That's two dollars and sixty cents. Please deposit another forty cents."

I dig in my pockets. Nothing. "I don't have it!"

"I'm sorry but I can't connect you. Would you like to make a collect call?"

"No!"

"Please hang up then, and your change will be returned."

I plead and try to bargain with her, but it's a no go. I hang up and my money clatters back out.

All I need is forty more cents. I steel myself and approach a woman in a red leather coat. She looks like she'd have plenty of money. "I'm sorry to bother you," I say apologetically, "but I need to borrow forty cents to make a long-distance call to my grandmother."

She gives me a glare like I've made some indecent suggestion. "There's no soliciting in here," she snaps. "Can't you read the signs?"

"I'm not soliciting, I'm just asking to borrow forty cents. I can mail it back to you when I get home."

The man beside her pipes up. "You heard the lady, sweetheart. No begging. Go on, get out of here and stop bothering people."

I try five more times. It's hideously embarrassing. One guy won't even look at me. It's like I'm not even there. I finally give up and crawl away to the other side of the station. It's amazing, not having enough money to do what you need to do, and nobody caring at all. How many times did I do the same thing?

Mortified and humiliated, I plug in my music, pull out my English book and hunch over it, trying to disappear. *It'll be okay*, I tell myself. I've been late for supper before. It'll only be an hour.

It's dark by the time the next bus leaves the station and right in the middle of rush hour. There's an accident at the Morningside exit, and it takes ages to get by it. I don't bother to try to read anymore. I feel so sorry for myself I cry most of the way.

When we get to Kingston I just about plough people down rushing for a cab. It's started to pour and I'm dripping, but my throat is dry with panic. I don't tell the driver I only have $2.60. I'll get the money when I get home. By the time we pull into James Street it's nearly eight o'clock.

There's a police car parked under the street light in front of Ava and Avo's house. And that's Susan's car behind it.

"Somebody's in trouble," the driver says.

The police leave right away. I'm home safe, end of story. The cab takes off as soon the driver gets his money. Avo leaves too, I don't know for where. He hasn't said a word to me. Ava and Susan are furious. Ava's face is like stone.

"Where were you?"

"I went to Toronto. I didn't lie to you, Ava." But she won't even look at me. "I left a note. I just didn't tell you where I was going, because I didn't want to worry you."

"Because you knew I tell you not to go," she cries angrily. "Why did you go?"

"Just . . . for a visit. I would have been home earlier except I missed the bus, and I didn't have enough money for the phone to let you know I'd be late, and there was an accident on the 401."

"I hope you didn't do anything stupid," says Susan sternly.

"No, I didn't. I didn't talk to anybody—except a dog."

They wave their arms and shout and harangue, and I have to promise I won't try anything like it ever again. Finally Ava turns with a sigh and opens the fridge and starts bringing out food. That means the worst is over.

Pretty soon we're sitting at the table drinking tea. Susan gives me one more disapproving look. "Actually, I didn't come over because you'd disappeared," she says. "It was coincidence that I showed up in the middle of things. In fact, I was coming over with some good news. I don't feel much like sharing it with you, after the scare you've given everyone . . . but I'm sure your grandmother will want to hear it."

Turns out, the insurance company has offered to settle for one hundred and fifty thousand dollars. Ava's eyes widen. Susan says the lawyer thinks we should accept it. I know it'll be going into a trust fund and invested to pay for my expenses—Susan already explained all that to me. "The lawyer and your grandparents are the trustees," she says.

"What does that mean?"

"It means they need to approve any expenditures, until you're twenty-five. Then it's all yours."

Until I'm twenty-five? Is that fair? Shouldn't I be able to make the decisions on how the money is spent, considering what I went through to get it? Especially considering I have things to do, and I need to get going on them now, not when I'm twenty-five? My allowance probably won't even go up.

I keep my mouth shut, though, and eat the tomato soup and toast and cheese Ava puts in front of me. Susan is talking about signing things and setting up accounts. Ava looks worried and keeps saying to her, "I leave all that to you." I know they mean well. There's no point in my getting into it. I'm too tired to think right now anyway. I'm glowering like an ungrateful, sulky teenager, but inside I'm on automatic pilot.

When Susan goes home, Ava clears the table. "I run a bath for you. Then bed."

"Thanks, Ava." My voice sounds hollow in my ears. "I'm really, really sorry I made you and Avo worry."

"I know." She pats my arm. "I know you're a good girl. Even when you do bad things."

My eyes well up. I soak in the steaming bath until I catch

myself falling asleep. I climb out before I drown, and get into the fresh pyjamas Ava has put out for me. My heart is so heavy I can barely hold myself up.

How grateful I am to be safe and dry and warm and cared for. Jesus and his mother stare down from the wall at me. They look sympathetic. But in my head I am still on that hard park bench, my eyes on the door of the house that has shut me out forever.

I know that if I go again, it will destroy what spirit I have left. But I promised Wolfie I'd come back for him, and I'll keep my promise. I fall asleep murmuring to him, "Be patient, darling. Be a good boy and don't forget me. You be a good dog and I'll try to be a good girl."

Chapter 21

I'm dreading Christmas. Before, I always loved it so much, all the family getting together, the excitement and the presents. I don't know what Ava and Avo do about Christmas. They don't put up outside lights or anything.

About two weeks before, Ava calls me to the phone. She sounds funny. "What's the matter? Who is it?" I call back.

"Her. Your mother."

Omigod! But—oh—it's Krystal's mother, she means. Not my mother. I go down the hall and pick up the phone.

"What's this Mia stuff?" a woman's voice demands. "Why have you gone and changed your name for?"

None of your business, I almost snap back. "I felt like it. I'm different since the accident." I add, "I haven't heard from you in a long time."

If I'm trying to make her feel guilty, it works. "I sent you a birthday card," she says. She starts going on about how busy she is and how tough her life is. The new guy she's living with, Earl, has been laid off and he's looking for another job, so they haven't been able to leave town. She's got a job at a call centre and the hourly rate stinks but she's getting lots of hours. She'll have to work right through the holidays.

It takes ten minutes or so for her to wind down. I still haven't got a word in. I've got nothing to say to her anyway. "Put Momma back on, will you?" she says. "Bye, honey. Do your homework. Love ya."

And that's it. I listen in while Ava talks to her. Mostly she says yes and no. After she hangs up, I ask anxiously, "So she's not coming, is she?"

Ava shakes her head, her lips tight. "We manage better without her."

For sure we do.

"Are we going to get a tree, Ava?" I ask.

"What we want a tree for?" She shakes her head. "Too much money."

But I want a tree. We always had a tree. I saw them for sale outside No Thrills. Thirty dollars.

I call Loki and talk him into coming and helping me. It's the first time I've called him in a while. "What do you want a tree for?" he asks.

"Don't you people have any idea how to celebrate Christmas? You *have* to have a tree. Even if you're a pagan. In fact, even more so, if you're a pagan."

He grumbles, but he comes with me. Unfortunately they're not very nice trees, all wrapped up tight in net condoms. "Don't you have any little ones?" I ask the man selling them.

"That's all we got."

I limp around, sorting through them. "These are all too big."

"Let's go then," Loki says.

Then this other guy calls over, "You want a wee tree, girlie?"

"Girlie," he calls me, like in the *Blue Castle* book Susan gave me. He's got a cigarette in his mouth and an electric chainsaw in his hand. He picks up a Scotch pine that looks like it's been hit by lightning, branches torn off and needles all brown. Before I can say forget it, he's cut it in half. He holds up the top and his cigarette wags. "Ten bucks."

The top half isn't bad. In fact, it's a darling little tree. We borrow a shopping cart to wheel it home. When we come in the back door with it, Ava frowns.

"Don't worry, if you don't want it in the living room, I can keep it in my room," I say. "I just wanted a tree."

"Such a stubborn girl." She shakes her head. "But it is only a little tree. We make room. You take that shopping cart back, Raymond."

"Why? Nobody else bothers," he protests. Which is true—there's a trail of sick and dying yellow carts between here and the store.

"You bother, Raymond. Nice boy like you." She knows his real name. Maybe she has something else on him too, because he does as he's told. "All the way back," she calls after him.

I'm not sure what do with the tree, now I've got it. Ava says Avo will take care of it, and sends me out again to the drug store to pick up some things for her. When I come back, Avo has nailed boards to the bottom of the tree and set it on a little table. Next to it is a cardboard box of old ornaments, separated by cardboard dividers, like eggs. They're made of fragile coloured glass: balls, birds, stars, even musical instruments: a violin and a trumpet.

"A job for you to do." Ava picks up a rainbow-coloured bird with a real feather tail. "That was your favourite when you were only so small. You don't remember? I told you to hold it gently. You never broke it."

I manage to find presents for everybody, though not much, because I'm still only getting fifteen dollars for an allowance. I find quite a nice fleece scarf for Avo, black and brown checks, not too much money, and a big paisley shawl for Ava. I get another one for Susan while I'm at it, two birds, one stone. Loki—well, I'd like to buy him a new wardrobe to replace his droopy-drawer pants and sloppy tops, but he'd never wear anything I got him.

At school I signed up to help serve Christmas dinner at the old folks home around the corner. I'm supposed to be there by eleven on Christmas Day. After breakfast I phone Loki and make him walk with me. "What for?" he says, but he comes. I'm hardly even using a cane now, but the sidewalks are icy. I'm terrified I'll fall.

I got him a present after all. He's surprised, and embarrassed when I hand it to him. "I didn't get you nothin'."

"I never expected you to. It's not much, just to say thank you. You helped me a lot."

His face lights up when he sees what it is. "Friggin' cool." It's some soccer annual about British and European teams I found in the sale bin at Indigo. It's got a lot of stuff in it about Chelsea, the team he likes.

He looks so pleased I can't help myself—I reach out to hug him. He pulls back and I get a whiff of booze.

"Are you drunk?" I ask him, disgusted.

"Keep your shirt on. It was only a beer."

"On Christmas morning!"

"Nothin' else to drink in the house."

On the way to the residence I hang on to his arm so I won't slip. It's about twenty below but he doesn't have mitts. He doesn't seem to notice the cold. He won't even zip up his coat.

When we get there he tries to take off again, but they snag him for kitchen duty. I'm supposed to carry around corsages of plastic holly and poinsettias and pin them on the old people. Some of the old guys like it a lot when I lean over them. Jessica and Waterski Boy and some other kids I know from school are singing carols. They seem surprised to see me. "Should you be doing this?" Jessica asks when we start carrying around the dinner plates. "Aren't you afraid you'll drop one?"

What a nightmare that'd be. "I'm okay." I concentrate hard.

The old people put away a lot of turkey and pie and ice cream. There's more carols after the meal, but by then half of them are dozing in their chairs. I feel the same way. I can hardly stagger home.

Loki seems a lot happier now that he's stuffed with turkey. He's going on about the movie he saw on TV last night. "This sucker's gonna top himself but there's this angel—"

"*It's a Wonderful Life.*"

"What?"

"That's the title. *It's a Wonderful Life.*"

"Yeah, right. How'd you know?"

"Because they've shown it on TV every Christmas Eve since Jesus was born."

He looks disappointed. Now he can't tell me the rest of the plot. He tries to anyway.

"So, what would you like to do with your life, if you could do anything?" I interrupt him.

"Work at KFC and get all the chicken I can eat."

"No, really."

"Own my own skateboard park."

"No, really."

He glares. "That's really."

There's a dirty crust of trampled snow on the sidewalk, and I have to watch where I put my feet so I don't end up on my ass. My bad leg is dragging. I'd like to hold on to his arm again, but I'm afraid he'll just pull away. "Are you studying for exams?" I ask him.

"What are you talkin' about? It's holidays!"

But exams start just a couple of weeks after we go back to school. I've been studying hard. He should too, if he wants to get anywhere. But I don't say that. Instead I tell him something I've been saving up. "Hey, Loki, I called Krystal."

He keeps on walking, head down, like he's mad that I can't keep up.

I limp faster after him. "You told me to call her, remember? So

I did. And she's okay. I didn't talk to her but some guy who seems to be hanging around my mom's house says she's doing okay. In my body."

Finally he slows down a bit. I'm out of breath. "Just think of it like a movie, Loki. You know, like those movies where a guy turns into a dog or a Volkswagen or something? You wouldn't have any problem with that, I bet."

"That's a movie."

"Yeah, but where does the idea come from? Somebody thought of it. So maybe stuff like that has happened. I don't mean turning into a Volkswagen, but there's lots of stories where somebody is transported into somebody else's life, like in the middle of King Arthur's court or something."

His head comes up. He's just thought of some movie where a dead woman starts living inside Steve Martin. The rest of the way home, he tells me the whole thing. He even lets me take his arm.

When we get to the door, I tell him, "Thanks for coming with me."

"That's okay. Better than staying home."

Merry Christmas.

That night in bed I think about what my own family would be doing now. Baby Stacey is too little to really get into it. But I bet she's grown. And the guy I got on the phone when I called Mom's number, is he hanging around giving out Christmas presents?

And what's *she* doing—the one who's sitting in my body in the midst of this happy family gathering? I've been thinking lately that maybe she wasn't hurt as bad as me. Sounds like, from what that guy said on the phone, she survived the dive without ending up paralyzed. She might not have had a lot of broken bones like me. She's probably not still dragging around on crutches and canes. Maybe she's going out to parties with the gang. Maybe right now she's out dancing. With Nate.

Chapter 22

Susan takes me to the RioCan Centre in the west end for the Boxing Week sales. For her Christmas present to me, she wants to buy me a pair of boots. We're there for like hours. I try on every pair in the place in my size. "Pick any ones you want," she says. "They're all half off the last marked price."

The problem is, I can't find anything that fits. Some I can't even zip up over my calves. I get mad at Krystal all over again for her stubby little Mediterranean legs. Susan tries to calm me down. "Your legs are fine. Whose fault is it if they make all the boots to fit Paris Hilton? Nobody else can get into them either."

But I see a couple of girls trying on the skinny boots and tossing their hair in front of the mirror. They fit into those boots just fine. I'm getting really miserable until I find this one gorgeous pair, caramel leather, so soft and buttery I'd like to lick them. And they have four-inch Cuban heels. They started out really expensive, three hundred and eighty-five dollars, the kind I'd guilt Dad into buying me because he felt bad about the split-up. The miracle is, they've been marked down three times already, so they're as cheap as anything I've tried on, eighty-five dollars. It's like a sign.

The tag says they're size eight but it's wrong. They're way

smaller than that, more like size six and a half. I zip them up and presto—Cinderella! I'm almost my right height again.

I've got to have them.

"Are you sure?" Susan says doubtfully, watching me stagger around in front of the mirror.

"I'm sure." She'll have to knock me down to take them off me.

"They do look amazing on you," she admits. "But with those heels, they'll be hard to walk in. I suppose you could ask your physiotherapist to order you some orthotics. The trust fund will pay."

I wear the boots out of the store. I see us reflected in the store window as we leave. When we came in, I was short. Now I'm as tall as Susan.

"Would you like to have dinner at my house?" she asks. "We can call Ava and let her know." It's just the two of us, because her husband is away in England for a couple of days. I never even knew where Susan lived before. It's in a part of town I haven't been to, close to the hospital, but I wasn't getting around much then. A lot of the houses in her neighbourhood are old, but hers is modern architecture. "Actually, it's fifty years old," she says.

"I didn't know they built things like this back in those days."

She smiles. "'Those days' is when I was born. It wasn't quite the dark ages."

The inside seems old, though, with antique furniture and oriental carpets. The floors are shiny wood, and the walls are covered in big paintings and quilts in brilliant colours with words embroidered on them, probably by somebody famous. Nothing is worn or ugly or sad. It doesn't smell like cabbage.

The kitchen is really nice, not all steel and granite countertop like Mom's, but cozy and bright with a big window looking out into the garden. It's less messy than I would have expected, considering the state of Susan's purse. "I'm a tidy cook," she says. "It's the one place in my life where I go at exactly the speed I want, one step at a time. Very calming. I hope you like Indian food."

Something soft brushes against my leg, and I look down into the green eyes of a black cat. It's like a tiny panther, with a wedge-shaped head. It meows and lets me pet it.

"You're special," Susan says. "Shiva is particular with her attentions. She doesn't warm up to just anyone." She puts on some rice and puts a big covered pot into the oven to heat, then takes a bunch of vegetables out of the refrigerator to make a salad. "You want a glass of wine?" she asks, like I'm an adult friend.

"That'd be great."

"White okay?" She takes a bottle from the fridge and pours some into two long-stemmed glasses.

"Do you have any pictures from when you were in India?" I ask her.

Her face lights up. "Funny you should ask. I just finished getting together all my old slides and having them put on a CD. I guess it was talking to you about it that made me finally get around to it."

"Can I see them?"

"You really want to? My family all groans if I even mention India."

"Yeah, I do."

She dries her hands, then turns on the laptop on the counter. I settle in front of it with my glass of wine, looking at Susan's pictures as she chops vegetables.

The backgrounds are bleached to pale brown by the sun, but the people are all in brilliant colours, turquoises, yellows, hot pinks. Most of them are girls and little children. In one picture half a dozen girls stand together carrying babies. Two of the girls are foreigners, and I pick out Susan right away, even though she's so young. Her hair is a lot darker than it is now and she's tanned, but she's still a lot lighter-skinned than the local girls. Their eyes are black, their teeth bright white.

Susan was skinnier then too, but almost everyone in these pictures is skinny. The cows are racks of bones.

"Why did you like India so much?" I ask.

"That I could be a different person than I was at home," she says promptly. "Nobody knew me. I came with no baggage. Nobody knew who my family was. Nobody knew what town I came from, where I went to school. They didn't know what Canada was like. They had no idea what to think of me except that I must be rich. I wasn't rich, but I had so much more than they did. I've never forgotten that."

"How long did you stay?"

"Two years. Which is a long time when you're that age."

"Why did you go home?"

"It was expected."

"At least you could go home. I can't."

She doesn't say anything for a bit. When she does, she asks me if I'm hungry.

"Starving."

She gets me to light some candles in the dining room and serves up our plates. "I hope I didn't make it too spicy. I cut back on the chillies."

"No, it's delicious." It really is. "Ava is a good cook too, but I like Indian food. There's this place near Yonge and St. Clair I used to go to with my friends if somebody had a birthday or something."

"O Calcutta." We both say it at once. Our eyes meet.

"Yeah, that's the one. You ever go there?"

She nods.

"I only ever got the butter chicken." The cat jumps up in my lap.

"Shiva!" says Susan. "Just lift her down." But I don't.

We talk some more about stuff. How she met her husband when she was travelling but they didn't get married until a lot later when they were both older and divorced from other people.

"Did anyone else in your family ever go to India?" I ask.

"Nobody. They've never understood why I loved it. Why I've kept going back there, five times."

"Your soul's journey," I say. "It probably has something to do with that."

"I think so too. It changed how I saw life. It changed the course of my life."

"Changed it so that one day you'd meet me?"

She smiles. "Maybe."

After dinner, when she starts to take me home, I remember I still haven't given her back her *Blue Castle* book. "I think I know why you gave it to me now. I'm supposed to live the life fate hands me and then everything will turn out fine."

"That's not why I gave it to you. It was just because it's a comfort-food kind of book. Keep it as long as you like."

"Maybe you want me to have my own Blue Castle."

"Maybe we all need one."

The Blue Castle is the fantasy place that the main character, Valancy, has where she goes in her mind when her awful life is too much to bear. I point out that it seems like Valancy's life got all straightened out in a year. Mine's going to take a lot longer.

Chapter 23

Exams start halfway through January. I study until I'm cross-eyed, and Ava marches in wearing her nightgown and wags her finger at me. But it's the first big chance I've had to show that former Goth slag Krystal Marques can do it, and I don't want to blow it. By the time I write the last exam, I'm pretty sure I've done okay.

Turns out I'm right—my marks are mostly in the high eighties. And a ninety-six in math! I never used to be that good.

The guidance guy, Mr. Mallen, calls me in. "You've really turned yourself around, Krystal." He seems puzzled. "Not many people manage it."

"My name has been changed to Mia on the school records since last September."

"Sorry. Mia, I mean." He apologizes to me! And I notice the way he talks to me is different from the way it was, more respectful. I still get angry thinking how sneering and patronizing he was that first time. Not so much for me, I can take care of myself. But Krystal didn't need that crap.

"You'll have to start thinking about what you're going to do once you graduate," he says.

I politely remind him I already told him last summer I was

thinking about it, and now I've decided. In my Amy days, I figured I'd take politics and economics or maybe development studies, and then work overseas for a while. But I've been reading up on all the scholarships Regi has that I can apply for, and there's a big one for the commerce program at U of T, the Adela Fererra Scholarship in Business for Catholic Portuguese girls. That's what I'll aim for. I know I've got the insurance money, but I don't want to spend all of it on school. I want to keep as much of it in reserve as I can. I may need it.

I thought it would be illegal to say what religion and nationality and gender a scholarship is for, but I guess if you're giving your money away, you can give it to Buddhist Abominable Snowmen if you want. It's your money—or in this case, Adela Fererra's. Anyway, I'm a Portuguese girl now, and Ava says I was baptized a Catholic. She has the certificate to prove it. I'll even go to mass with her and light a candle to seal the deal.

After that dreadful day in Toronto, I promised Susan I wouldn't try to contact anyone from my old life, that I'd live the life I'm in. I made a pact with myself too: to do nothing until I can walk without a limp and until I have a plan. I've tried not to even think about Mom or Nate or anybody else I love, because it makes me sad and crazy. When I get really, really down, I still use the phone card to call my old cellphone and listen to my friends' messages. I don't do it much, though. I'm only on the second card.

Amy, if you can hear this, babe, I love you . . . I'm missing you something awful. I'm praying for you, Ame. The team sends their love. We're not the same anymore. Hurry back.

And then Nate. *I just wanted to hear your voice. I wish I could have—I wish—I'd give anything . . .*

Over and over, over and over. Nate, I'd give anything too.

There's never anything new, of course. I listen to the old messages and save them, listen and save. And then one lousy February day, standing in the dark hallway in the empty house,

I punch in as usual. And hear *You have no new messages. No saved messages.*

It's like I've been kicked in the stomach. They're gone? My messages are gone? How can that be?

I clutch the phone and redial. Still my voice: *Hi, it's Amy, leave a message.* But no messages. Not one.

"Nobody's got the right to do that!" I howl. "Those were mine! They were all I had left!" I shriek, I pound the wall with my fists. Finally I crawl into bed and lie there, my heart pounding. What does it mean? Who did that?

It's a dark, dark day.

I can't leave it alone. Next day in my spare, I use the phones outside the main office. My voice is still telling me to leave a message, and somebody's left a new one, somebody I don't even know. It means *she* must be using it. Krystal's using my voice and my voice mail. She's giving out my number to people I don't know. I delete the message. I don't want her to notice I've hacked in.

I start calling every day, from the pay phone at school, from the one outside No Thrills, but she never picks up. She doesn't get that many messages, and they aren't from anybody I know. But one time it's somebody changing a doctor's appointment and I skip it, don't delete. I leave it for her, which is a mistake.

Through one thing or another, she must notice something's going on, because she changes her password. I can't get in anymore.

I'm frustrated and furious with her. She's not going to get away with it! What would she use for a new password: Her birthday? Mine? Her old locker combination? The name of some Goth group?

Finally on Saturday afternoon Ava goes out, and I try to crack the code. Ten minutes max, I get it. Her old initials and a spare: KMMM. Too easy, really—she's not that smart. And no new messages, after all that. She's not that popular either.

Now I know she's alive and functioning, I'm so pissed at her all the time. Like she's the enemy. Like she took my life, my mom, my home. Like it's her fault. Sometimes, though, I wonder how she's doing, and it's all I can do not to leave a message myself: "Hi, Krystal, it's Amy, remember me? I'm at your grandparents. Call me, okay? Say hi to Mom and Wolfie." What stops me is I'm afraid she'd change her number altogether, and I don't want to lose that.

The other reason is the vow I made to myself of no contact until I have a plan, and I don't have one. I lie in bed at night and think: There has to be a way. Some way to reverse what happened, to set up everything just right so we can throw the switch to get us back to our right bodies. But who's got the manual for that? Who can I ask? If it worked one way, doesn't it have to work in reverse too?

Do we have to die again?

Winter in this place is so ugly, I can't believe people survive it. Every day on my way to school and back, some jerk splashes me with slush. I wear my lovely boots, but they're not allowed in class. They have to stay in our lockers, all the sludge and filth off the streets sitting in a swamp at the bottom. Boots aren't part of the uniform—like fifty pounds of white, goose-pimply thigh are.

Finally, after about a thousand years, it starts to feel like spring. Crows caw to each other in the tops of trees, blackened snowbanks melt into the sewers. The sidewalks are clear enough so I can walk down to the river to check whether the ice has broken up in the bay. Every day there's more open water out in the middle of the channel. Then one day it's all open, the ice completely gone. The Canada geese are back at the club dock. They can't have migrated that far.

I get Shelley to snoop around at school and find out for me when the rowing club starts on the river. I've kept away from there since the day I ran into Tracy and Helen, the two rowers from the Regi crew. Once back in November I saw Tracy in the hall, recognized her by her strawberry-blond hair and her height, and she recognized me. She didn't say anything, just shook her head. At the time it freaked me out, but I've started to think, how's she going to prove anything anyway? She can ask me anything about rowing or our crew at Lawrence Park. I'll tell her. She can ask how our club did at the Henley regatta and I'll give results. I can tell her how Alison Gendron got scouted by Washington State and who on our team has her sights set on getting to the nationals. Actually, it's all on the club's website. How's anyone going to figure out the truth in a million years?

So on the start-up day in April, I'm sitting on a bench in the pale afternoon sun, watching the rowers carry the boats to the water. They're all whooping and cheering. When they fit the oars and push off from the dock, I want to be out there with them so bad I can taste it. And I'm going to do it.

The last time I saw the physio, I asked if I'd be okay to row. I'm walking so much better I never use the brace now. "Your upper body damage is pretty well repaired," she said. "Your pelvis and legs took the big hit. You'll still need to be careful with your back, but it's healing well." She looked at me over her glasses. "Just go slow for once."

She knows that coach I met last fall. "Mike trained a couple of my patients for rowing in the Special Olympics," she says. "Both of them paraplegics. He knows what he's doing."

One day I'm casually limping past the open door of the boat-sheds, and when I see Mike heading to the dock, I wave. He comes over, big smile. "Hey, there. Haven't seen you since last fall. You're moving much better."

"Thanks. I've been working on it. I got rid of my crutches at Christmas."

"That's terrific. Well, keep it up." He starts to walk away.

I call after him. "Do you think I could row?"

He stops, looks surprised. "Row? You'd have to ask your doctor that question. You said you had spinal injuries."

This isn't good. He's not nearly as encouraging as he was before. I remember telling him I used to be taller. Of course, that didn't have anything to do with my spine.

"If you mean row recreationally," he goes on, "get medical clearance and just sign up. But if you're asking if you can row with the club, competitively, I have no idea." He looks me frankly up and down. "Regi already has a couple of strong spares. And they're tall."

I know I'm way too short. My heart sinks.

"Even if you were 100 percent recovered, you wouldn't be a good match. But . . ." He's silent for a moment, I guess seeing I'm not taking this well. "Have you ever coxed?"

I shake my head despondently. "I've never tried."

"You're the right size, if you lose a little weight. Think you'd be any good at it?"

I stammer. "I, uh—don't know." His remark about my weight stings. There's nothing wrong with my weight, for a human being. For a coxie, though, the thing is to weigh as little as possible and still be alive and breathing.

"What are you doing right now?" He grabs a life jacket off a pole and when I nod, throws it to me. I follow him to the dock.

I scramble awkwardly into the bow of the aluminum runabout. He unties it and starts the motor. We zoom out. And I'm on the water. It's miraculous to be feeling the spray on my face, smelling it, feeling the ripples beneath the hull.

Mike shouts through the megaphone: "Pick it up there, number two!"

It's a perfect golden spring afternoon, warm and still. I hear the coxies giving the counts: "Ten to build, ten to hold, ten to lengthen . . ." And "Get your butt into it, number four!" It's like I'm in the boats with them. I feel the pain in my shoulders, the rush of lactic acid in my muscles.

They're good, these girls. But I see the problems, too.

"Concentrate! You're rushing your slide!" Mike calls out. In between, he talks to me about coxing. "The stroke sets the pace, but the coxswain has to call the shots."

Well, I know that.

When we head into shore and I manage to climb out onto the dock, he asks me, "So what do you think?"

I stop myself from falling on my knees and begging. "I think I'd like to try," I gulp.

"Good. Come by a little early tomorrow, around four. We'll go out again."

I fly all the way home.

Chapter 24

I'm there the next afternoon and the afternoons after that. I start coxing in my sleep: *Ten to lengthen, rate up in two, push for the stride! Three seat, get in time!* After half a dozen times out with Mike, he says, "Regi is down a coxie in the fours. You good to start?"

So there I am getting up at five thirty again three mornings a week, just like in my old life, and trundling down to the boatsheds. Avo and Ava don't like me being on the street in the dark, and the first couple of times Avo gets up and walks with me. But I convince him it's the safest time: all the drunks are asleep and the burglars have packed it in. The only people out are runners, dog people, and rowers.

The four girls in my boat are Lynsey, Alex, Keri, and Julie. They're happy to have a warm body in the coxie's seat, so we get along fine. When everybody goes up for breakfast to Tiffin's, the café near the sheds, they ask me too. But I don't go, because I might run into Tracy and Helen there. They row eights, and so far I'm managing to avoid them.

I tell myself not to worry. I'm just so happy being out on the water again, even if I'm not rowing. And sometimes if I'm lucky, if I time it right, I do manage to get in a quick row by myself in a single. It's lovely. But I'm not strong enough to carry a boat myself, so I have to be on the spot when somebody brings one in and find somebody else to help me get it back to the shed.

I'm into the routine, and things go great—until the end of May. That's when I let Lynsey and Alex talk me into rowing with one of the eights. "We've got two away and one of the subs can't make it," Lynsey says.

"I'm a coxie, not a rower."

"Mike said to ask you. And I've seen you rowing on your own."

I know it's a bad idea. I shake my head.

"Come on, Mia," Alex says. "Help us out of a spot."

Against my better judgment, I say okay. Always a sucker for coming to the rescue.

"We'll take it slow to start," their coxie promises.

I adjust the blocks for my short legs. I'm so nervous. I know this is crazy. None of it feels right. They've been running and weight training right through the winter. I don't have any muscle mass at all. I used to row in seventh seat and now I'm rowing in fourth, which feels extremely weird. How am I going to hold it together?

But we glide out onto the bay, and the sound and smell of the water fill my head. The tension lifts as I feel that old adrenalin rush. Right then I know it's going to be fine.

I focus on the knobs of Lynsey's spine ahead of me. Our oars sweep the surface in calm unison. My shoulder muscles respond. My abs tighten. It's not easy—I'm really going to be stiff tonight. I haven't done this in a long time. My arms are shorter than anyone else's. But miraculously I'm doing okay.

Those first few strokes are great. But the miracle is about to expire.

Out of the corner of my eye I see the other crew of eights come up behind us—Tracy and Helen's team. Our stroke picks up the pace and we surge ahead. But it's too late, I've already lost it, lost the rhythm. I try to focus, fix my eyes on the curling hairs on the back of Lynsey's neck. But it's gone.

"Number four! You're rushing your slide."

"Number four! You're missing your catch!"

I hear muttering. The blade of my oar catches the oar behind me. The crack travels like an explosion up my arm.

Someone swears.

"Come on, Mia, get with it," Alex says. But I can't get with it. It's like I've never rowed before, like this body has never rowed. My oar is tangled with the ones ahead and behind me, like pick-up sticks. The boat swerves and rocks wildly. Everybody is screaming at me.

"Okay, start again," Coxie says grimly. But it's no good, I know it. I've lost the rhythm and I won't get it again.

Coxie roars: "Mia, lift your oar!"

Ignominiously, face burning, I lift my oar out of harm's way. My shame is visible for everyone to see. To a chorus of catcalls from the next boat, we head back to the dock.

"What happened?" Coxie yells furiously at me as I lift myself out of the boat. "Mike said you could row."

I can't even speak. It's over. I stumble up the dock. Now they know I'm an impostor. I have to haul my butt out of here and never come back. Outside the boatshed I see Mike, standing, watching. I pray for the earth to open and swallow me up.

"Mia!" I hear steps behind me. I quicken my pace.

"Mia, stop." Someone grabs my shoulder. "What happened out there?"

I turn and see it's Lynsey. I try to pull away from her. "I lost it."

Her round, kind face is puzzled. "But you were rowing fine to begin with."

"I just couldn't keep it up. I can't row anymore."

A yell comes from the second boat. "Told you she was lying."

Lynsey turns around. "Oh, shut up! Keep out of it."

"She was nearly killed by a truck, remember?" somebody else shouts. "See how well you can row after that, Tracy Stevens."

Lynsey's arm goes around my shoulders. "Don't sweat it, Mia. Try again tomorrow. You'll be okay."

I can't believe she's being so nice to me.

I shake my head. "No. I just can't do it."

"Don't give up. Don't be a quitter. I've seen you rowing a single. You're good."

"Not good enough. You've got better subs. Give them the chance."

And I walk away. I skirt the boatshed and Mike and head home. Shower, change my clothes, and hurry off to school.

All day long I try not to think about it. The only good thing is that I don't run into anyone from the club in the halls. I won't ever row on a team again. That's gone. I'll cox, if they still want me, but when I row, I'll row alone.

Next morning I have to go back and cox the fours like usual. It just about kills me. But nobody tries to stop me. Nobody says a thing about my humiliation yesterday. We act like it never happened.

But that's not the end of it.

A couple of days later I'm in the changing room when I hear somebody come in behind me. As usual I'm last, because I'm slowest. I turn around to see who it is, and there's Tracy sitting on the bench.

My mouth goes dry. She's already changed, she's just waiting. For me. I keep my head down, lace up my shoes. I have to walk past her to get to the door.

She stands and steps in front of me. She's big, and her eyes are hard as rock. "So what's going on, *Krystal*?"

I try to duck around her. "My name's Mia."

"I know who you are, *Krystal*. My sister's in your science class. She says you're lying. No way you're from Toronto. You haven't moved here from anywhere. You're Krystal Marques who was in that accident. You just changed your name."

I try again to get past, but she's nearly six feet and built like a block of wood. The freckles stand out on her nose. "What do you care?" I squeak.

"I don't like being lied to."

I don't have a strategy, and that's a mistake. I do the only thing I can think of at short notice.

I go berserk.

"Why won't anybody ever give me a chance?" I yell. I squirt tears. I feel my face flame scarlet. "No matter what I do, I'll always be that little slut Krystal. That screw-up. I'm sick of it. I don't *want* to be Krystal anymore."

Tracy steps back.

I ratchet up the volume. "It's not fair! It's not fair!" I shriek. "Why can't I have a chance like everybody else?"

The door opens, and Lynsey and Keri from my boat push in, mouths open in amazement. Tracy's friend Helen is there too.

"What the hell's going on?" Keri asks. They look from one to the other and draw a quick conclusion: Tracy's bullying me. Keri rushes over to me. "What did you do to her, Tracy? What's the matter, Mia?"

"I didn't do anything to her!" Tracy scowls. "I just told her I know she lied to everybody. She never rowed for the Argonaut club. She never lived in Toronto for one second. She lives on James Street." But she doesn't sound as mad as before, more defensive. "All I want is for her to tell the truth."

Lynsey and Keri look confused. "Uh, I don't get it," says Keri.

"She told me and Tracy she used to row at Lawrence Park," Helen explains.

"And a bunch of other crap," says Tracy. "None of it true. She's Krystal Marques, that girl who used to hang out with the Goth losers. I knew I'd seen her before."

They're all staring at Tracy like she's crazy. "Mia? A *Goth*? But she rows!"

"Tracy's right," I pipe up, snuffling a bit. "I was a Goth. But that was before. I wanted my life to be different. I'm sorry if I lied, but I didn't do it to hurt anybody." The tears start to flow again. Lynsey pats my shoulder.

Helen frowns, puzzled. "But how did you know all that stuff about the regattas and everything? You couldn't have just made it up. You knew what you were talking about."

I think fast. "My, uh, cousin. My cousin Amy, in Toronto, she rows. I wanted to be like her. I wished I could have her life."

"Amy who?" Helen asks.

"Wexford."

"Amy . . . and she rows for Lawrence Park." Helen thinks for a moment. "What does she look like? Blond? Tall?"

"Yeah."

"Lightweight or heavyweight?"

"Lightweight. We don't look anything the same. You'd never know we were related."

"Oh, right." She's got it now. "*Amy*. Remember her, Tracy?"

Tracy nods. "Oh, yeah, *Amy*. She's your *cousin*?" She peers into my smeary face. "You're right about not looking like her. She's good, Amy," she tells the others. "Can she row! And majorly focused—don't get in her way, eh, Helen?"

"Well, you'll never row anything like her, Mia," says Helen. "Even when you're 100 per cent recovered. You don't have the build. You'd have to train for years to be any good. You might as well forget it."

"But she's a good coxie," says Alex. "Better than we had."

"That's surprising," says Helen.

"Even Mike says so," says Lynsey.

"Coach's pet," grumbles Tracy.

"Come on, let's go eat," says Alex. "If we don't get there in two minutes, Tiffin's kitchen will be shutting down. Come on, Mia, move it."

I follow them up to breakfast. I'm starving.

So everything's great now. I watch them eat their whole-wheat bagels and peanut butter, and I eat my low fat yogourt, happy just to be there. Now I don't have to hide, I don't have to keep out of anybody's way. Tracy shakes her head whenever she sees me, but it's no big deal.

Rowing's a lot different for me now, though. In the old days, coach used to say to us, "You have room in your life for three things. School and family are two—and you choose the other thing. If it's not rowing, you shouldn't be here."

Rowing used to be my other thing. But I have a different one now, and it's not the third thing in my life, it's the whole thing.

Part IV

Two Years On

Getting Back
Where I Belong

Chapter 25

A lot happens in the next two years. Not enough, of course. I don't come out looking much more like Amy Wexford than when I started. I've grown an inch and a half and my hair's a little blonder, thanks to more streaks. I've kept at the physio, working on my bad side. I still limp when I'm tired, but I'm working on that too.

I go on coxing the fours. They love me. Tracy doesn't bother me. Helen is embarrassingly nice, because she feels sorry for me. I row the single scull when I get a chance—not competitively, but to blow off steam. It's still great being in a boat, on my own or with the team, but if I can't row like I used to, I'm not interested. I've got my other thing, my third thing, my whole thing, to do.

I manage to hold a friendship together with Loki, barely. He says I'm on his case all the time about school and marks, but somebody has to be. His family doesn't know he's alive. One day he comes up to me all excited because he's got a job at the A&P loading groceries on the shelves at night, seven to midnight.

"Brilliant—you're already too tired during the day to stay awake at school."

"I need the money," he scowls. "Nobody's going to give me

any scholarship. Or fancy trust fund."

"What do you need the money for?"

"Maybe I'll try to get into Ryerson."

"Ryerson!" I'm surprised. "It'd be a lot cheaper to take a course here."

"That's not what you're doing, is it?"

Another summer passes, another fall, and I'm on the home stretch. By June I'll be out of Regi, baccalaureate program and all. Maybe I'm not in the top of my class in physics and chemistry, but I've been pulling off nineties in law and commerce. The competition is fierce, and I want that four-year scholarship. I've applied to commerce programs at three schools: Queen's, McGill, and Toronto, but Toronto is the only one I want, the one Adela Fererra's scholarship is for.

The wait to hear back is excruciating. In May the replies finally come. Ava is so proud: I'm accepted at all three! I know she wants me to go to Queen's, and so does Susan, but that's not part of my plan.

And Adela Fererra comes through.

On Labour Day Susan drives me to university in Toronto. My pitiful possessions only take up half her trunk space. They fit into three suitcases. My trust fund, thank god, bought me a laptop.

Susan helps me carry everything up to my dorm room on the third floor. I asked for a single, but I'm going to have to share. The residence halls are in chaos, lost souls and their parents everywhere. The double room is tiny, like a prison cell. We make up my bed with the new sheets and duvet Susan and I bought at Ikea. I set up my pictures of Ava and Avo on the desk—one Susan took of the three of us, and a copy of the one taken on their wedding day.

Susan looks over at the other bed, two feet away from mine. "It'll be tough for you, being an only child," Susan says.

"It'll be worse if I hate my roommate." And if she wants to party when I want to study. If she leaves her underwear on the floor.

We've just finished unpacking when there's a knock on the door. It's my roomie and her dad, each with a laundry basket of stuff. We introduce ourselves: she's Alison Bradley. She looks around the tiny room. "Wow," she says. We all nod. Not much space.

She doesn't seem hateful. She's from Orillia, and she seems like a nice girl, round-faced and sort of wholesome, with curly dark hair.

We leave her and her dad to it and walk down to the car together to say goodbye. Susan looks like she's winding up to say something, but she only hugs me. "I think I'm going to cry," she says, pulling handfuls of Kleenex out of her bag. "It must be menopause. Bye, darling. I'll email you when I get home."

I stand in the parking lot and wave goodbye. It's funny, I'm sort of crying too, when all I should be thinking is: I made it! I did it! I'm back in Toronto where I've been longing to be, hardly a mile away from my mother and my home—and what I'm feeling is homesick for James Street. Avo kissed me on both cheeks. Ava went back into the house because she didn't want me to see her weeping. It's crazy, but I wish I was back there.

Maybe I'm scared, being so close.

I walk slowly back up to the dorm room. Alison and her dad are still carrying in loads. I'm grateful she isn't horrible, but I wonder how I'm going to manage. There's no privacy even to think. It's all so noisy. People slam doors, play music, and yell to each other up and down the corridors. They stand under our windows and drink and shout. That night I lie in bed and listen to Alison breathe across the narrow space. I could reach out and touch her head.

"You're awake, aren't you?" she says suddenly, startling me. She sits up and looks at the clock. "It's two thirty," she says. "They'll quiet down soon."

The next days are all initiation stuff. We shuffle around like lost lambs behind some second-year know-it-all. I'm still homesick.

I miss Ava bringing me cups of tea with cookies while I study. I miss Avo dumping funny-looking vegetables in the sink. I try to make the best of it and to be cheerful around Alison. She doesn't seem to be minding the chaos that much. She didn't ask to be stuck with some depressive.

I hold it together with her for forty-eight hours. She's nice, but she's messy. She leaves her stuff on the floor where we both trip over it. It's not rocket science to realize that won't work. I sit her down for a talk. "I don't want to be a bitch, Alison, but it'll be easier for us both if we agree on some rules." I say it as nicely as I can.

She has these big, scared eyes that get bigger the longer I talk. Her face has gone bright red. "I would have put my stuff away but there's no room," she says defensively.

To be honest, I feel kind of bad, picking on her. I know she must be homesick too. But it has to be done. So I show her how she can organize things, which she hasn't a clue about. At least we get her things out of all the boxes and garbage bags and onto shelves. And at the end of it she's still speaking to me.

Next day we go to Honest Ed's to buy storage containers for under our beds. It's actually quite fun, doing things with her, and for an hour I don't think more than a couple of times about the phone call I'm about to make, the one I've been thinking about for two years. Alison's having a tough time finding her way around. I like being able to help her. I know the shortcuts—I used to walk through the campus on Philosopher's Walk all the time with my friends. I always thought it was romantic. It's not so much now, crowded with excited students.

Fortunately, Toronto doesn't go for quite as much of that ra-ra-ra orientation crap like they do in Kingston at Queen's, no purple people running around slapping three hundred-dollar leather jackets on the street. By Thursday it's mostly over. Alison gets a ride home to Orillia at noon. I go back to residence and make my call.

Not that I really expect to get through. It's been months since

I've tried the number. She could have changed it by now. And told Mom and the guy who answered the phone that time not to give her new one out.

But it rings. *Hey, it's Amy. Leave your number and I'll get back to you.* I can't believe it's still the same message, my message. So what does that mean?

I take a deep breath and instead of just hanging up, I leave a message. I'm so nervous it comes out as a sort of a croak. "I'd rather call you Krystal, if you don't mind. Return my call, would you?" I leave her my number. "And call me Mia."

The evening passes. No call back. Another day, and I begin to sweat. Maybe she doesn't want any contact. Or maybe she didn't make it after all. Maybe nobody had the heart to cut off her phone. That day I sneaked away to Toronto, I saw Mom but no sign of her. Maybe she was in a hospital somewhere. Maybe she still is.

I spend the weekend alone in a crazed state, my door shut, waiting. I try to be patient and keep my mind on other things. I don't have any work for classes yet, so I read my texts. On Sunday afternoon I'm propped on my bed with *Introduction to Business Economics*, not absorbing a single word. I'm despairing. What am I going to do next? This wasn't part of my plan. It's not much of a plan, I admit, but it's all I've been able to come up with so far.

The phone rings. I leap out of bed, telling myself, *Don't get excited. It's probably Susan calling to check in.*

But I recognize the number on the call display and it's not Susan's. I swallow hard and pick up.

"Um, Mia?" A girl's voice, a little husky.

"Krystal?"

There's a long pause. Then: "This is Amy."

"Krystal, you mean."

"I'm Amy now."

"No, you're not. I'm not ever calling you Amy."

"Everybody else does."

After two years I finally get through to the woman who's living in my body, and we're squabbling like ten-year-olds! Any second she'll hang up on me. "Thanks for calling back," I say quickly. "I was afraid you wouldn't."

"Sorry about that." She doesn't sound sorry. "We were at the lake."

"We." "At the lake"—my lake. At my cottage. "Don't you have classes?"

"I'm not in school. Where are you? You have a Toronto number."

"At U of T, in res. We need to talk."

Longer pause. "Why?"

I don't know what I'm hearing in her voice: suspicion? Fear? Why would she want to see me? She's got everything she didn't have in her lousy Krystal life—a mom, a family, a nice place to live, a lake. Why should she risk all that by admitting that I exist?

I'm betting on just one thing—that she's as lonely as I ever was. As I am. That we're the only two in the universe who understand what we've been going through.

"What do you want, anyway?" she asks.

"Nothing." At least, not yet. "I just thought it might help us if we talked."

I hear her let her breath out. "Okay," she says finally. We arrange to meet three days from now, on Wednesday, at the Starbucks nearest to the Davisville subway. That's the earliest she can manage.

"How will I know you?" I ask.

"I'm—" Then she gives a sort of squeak and laughs nervously. "Oh, I get it." She makes her voice stern. "Just don't try and pull anything, or you'll be sorry," she says. Tough girl.

"And what exactly do you think I could pull?"

On Wednesday I come out of the subway in my old neighbourhood for the first time since that long-ago PD Day. I feel sick to my stomach. Force myself to cross the street.

I'm standing in line at Starbucks waiting to pick up a coffee when this tall, beautiful girl, maybe five-nine, five-ten, comes in. She's wearing a striped top and skinny black jeans, and she has the most amazing straight black hair. She orders a skim-milk chai latte. "No sugar."

The funny thing is, hair and all, I know it's her, but she doesn't recognize me.

"Krystal?"

She turns and sees me. She screams.

Chapter 26

Every head in the place swivels. You could hear a pin drop. She forces a smile with brilliant white teeth. "I didn't recognize you. You look—"

"Amazing."

"Yes." Her eyes are practically popping out of her head. "You do look amazing. Not how I expected."

I collect my coffee. "I'll get us a seat." I sound calm but my hands are shaking. I can barely hold onto the cup.

When she slides into the booth across from me with her tea, it's like looking into a mirror, except I know I never looked that good. Eyes like bits of summer sky, wide shoulders, ivory skin—you can see she doesn't get outside much. She's wearing black eyeliner, but I would not call the effect Goth.

I point. "The hair."

"Yeah, well. I don't do blond."

"What does Mom think of it?"

She smiles faintly. "She didn't like it at first, but she hasn't said anything about it lately. You look really different from—from what I expected. From how I used to, you know. Even—" she laughs nervously—"a bit like me. Me now."

"Only shorter. Quite a change, eh? I had to work at it."
Whereas you, I don't say, *got a great body in top condition.*

She drops her eyes, stirs her chai like it has lumps in it. "I don't know what to say next. What do you want?"

People are still sneaking looks at us, wondering if one of us is going to scream again. I keep it light. "I'm not sure. Just to talk, you know, to start off. Like, how are you? I tried to find out but I couldn't. I mean, you look fine."

She waves her hand. "Yeah, I am. I had some, you know, brain swelling at first, and they put me in a medically induced coma, that's what they called it. That was like weeks. When I came out of it—well, you know."

I do. "It was awful."

She nods. "Yeah, awful. I was in traction too, because of my neck being almost broken. I thought I'd died and gone to hell. I mean, literally." She fumbles in her bag for her sunglasses and jams them on. I see her swallowing.

"You okay?"

"Sorry." Her voice wobbles. "I haven't talked to anybody about it before."

"Nobody?"

"Nobody. Do we have to, right now?"

"Not right now." But she hasn't asked how I am, how it was for me. Well, that can wait. "You're not at university?"

She sucks on her chai. "I'm taking some time off before I decide what I want to do with my life." The words comes out like she's said them before.

"Like—you *are* okay? Your head, I mean?"

"I'm not brain damaged, if that's what you mean. I just couldn't pick up where you left off."

I can imagine. "So what are you doing at the moment?" It comes out sounding corny and chatty, like we're girlfriends getting together for coffee to catch up.

"Just . . . some modelling."

"Modelling!" I'm stunned. Modelling? After all the hours and hours and hours I put into feeding and training that body so I could be the best rower on the team? After all the studying, the work, the cramming to get into UBC, which has the best rowing club in the country—what's she doing? Modelling! "How much bulimia do you think that makes you personally responsible for?"

"I don't diet." She goes all defensive. "I don't like it all that much, but it's something to do. And it pays well."

I start to say she doesn't need money, Mom and Dad have plenty of it. But I swallow it. Let it go. I can see why money would be important to her, after the life she had. There's so much else I want to know. "What about Wolfie? Is Wolfie still . . . ?" He's eight, old for a golden retriever. Suddenly I'm terrified of what she's going to say. I stuff my paper napkin over my mouth.

"Hey, take it easy. He's fine. He just can't go upstairs very fast anymore. Poor old Wolfie." She smiles. She likes him.

"Did he notice, I mean, the difference, after the accident?"

"Yeah, he did. Mom thought it was weird how he wouldn't have anything to do with me at first. She thought it was because he was mad at me for leaving him so long when I was in the hospital. But he knew. He knew I wasn't you."

"By 'Mom' I take it you mean my mother." I can't help sounding catty. I'm jealous. "So are you two close?"

The sarcasm goes right past her. "Mostly." She shrugs. "But you know how she is, so busy and everything. She was right there all the time I was in the hospital, though. And she's always saying how proud she is of me."

I hear something in her voice. "But it's not perfect, is it?"

Her eyes flash. "Maybe not, but it's okay. A lot better than I was used to."

"Right." I drink my cooling coffee. She stirs the froth on her chai latte.

"It's so weird, you living with my grandparents," she says after a pause. "They hated me."

"They never hated you. They came to Toronto to see you in the hospital. Of course, it was me they saw. Anyway, it's okay now. I've fixed it."

"You *fixed* it?" Now it's her turn to flare up. "Gee, thanks. And how about my mother? Did you fix her too?"

"Big fat zero there."

She tries to look like she couldn't care less, but her face gives her away.

"Well, not zero," I amend. "I shouldn't have said that. I heard she came to the hospital too, but I don't remember. She's called a couple of times. And she sent you a birthday card."

"But she hasn't been home to visit you? You haven't seen her?"

"No, and I don't want to. Have you tried to get in touch with her?"

"Why would I? That bitch dumped me. I don't care if I ever see her." Then she sighs. "I did try, once, but her number isn't listed. Probably so nobody could come after her for money she owes. She was always maxing out her credit cards."

She asks me about Loki—calls him Loco.

"He's Loki now. He's in Toronto too," I say. "He's at Ryerson. Doing the film program."

Her jaw drops. "Loco? Raymond? He's doing a film program? I don't believe it. You're kidding."

"Nope. It's true. You know how he was always crazy about movies."

"That's incredible. I wish I could see him," she says wistfully.

"Well, you could. He knows."

"He *knows*?" Her jaw drops. "He knows? Did you *tell* people? Are you crazy?"

"I tried to tell. Only two even half-believed me. Loki was one of them. I take it you never told?"

She shakes her head vehemently. "No, nobody! I told you, I just said I couldn't remember much. At first I hated everybody and everything, but then after a while . . ."

"Then you didn't want to go back to being Krystal."

"Yeah, well." She glares at me. "That's what you'd think, wouldn't you?"

She gets up and gets us water. Her face looks really drawn—beautiful, but drawn. "You look wiped," I say.

"So do you," she says. "Can we quit now?"

"For now."

We're already outside when I take a deep breath and ask the question I told myself not to. "You know, um, Nate?"

"Nate Dubinsky? Yeah." She's got her sunglasses on again, so I can't see her expression.

"How's he doing?"

"He's—" She bites her lip. "I don't know. Not so good for a while. I don't see him anymore."

"Anymore? You were seeing him?"

"Can we talk about this later?"

At least we're agreed there'll be a later.

"What do you want?" she asks again as we stand on the corner, me heading for the subway to go back to residence, her to go back to the house where I grew up.

"I'm not sure. What do *you* want?"

"For you not to ruin everything. I won't let that happen."

She says it again, to make sure I get the point.

Chapter 27

I wait on the subway platform, my mind churning. So what *do* I want from her? I want it all back—just what she doesn't want.

Whenever I'm trying to get to sleep at night, I have this story I make up in which I'm at the lake. Mom is there, and that guy who answered the phone. I've remembered now who he is: Greg, his name is, an old family friend who's now obviously more than that. And the old gang is all up there too, Gabby and Elly. And Nate.

And me. Not like before, but the way I am now. Actually, we're both there: me in Krystal's body, and Krystal in mine.

And Mom comes over to the two of us and says, "Who is this lovely young woman?"—meaning me. "I don't remember you, dear, but you seem very familiar. You and Amy could be sisters. Don't you think so, Greg?"

Yeah, right. Of course I've fallen down on that score. I really don't look anything like Amy, no matter how hard I've tried. For one thing, I'm five foot four. I can't wear heels all the time. But in this fantasy I'm taller and blonder and everybody thinks I'm fantastic, very cool and smart. This Greg guy asks me what I'm studying, and he's so impressed when I tell him I'm in the top of my class in commerce that he gives me his card and tells me to keep in touch—there's a job for me in his company when I graduate. I'm on my way to being practically a member of the family.

And then, in this fantasy, after everybody goes to bed, I walk down to the dock and sit on the end, my feet in the water. There's a full moon, its reflection making a wide golden path on the lake. Suddenly I hear footsteps and turn and see someone coming down the path. I know right away that it's Nate.

He steps out onto the dock. It's too dark to make out his face clearly but I can see his eyes in the moonlight. I stand and he puts his hands on my shoulders. His fingers are warm. "Who *are* you?" he asks. "I feel like I've known you before, but I know that can't be true."

I say nothing, just put my lips against his. In an instant we're all over each other. I slip my hands under his shirt so I'm touching his skin and he's touching mine. I never get much further with the details than that—I don't have that much experience. But all of a sudden, bingo, at that significant moment, I'm Amy again, like I've never been away.

Krystal is gone. She never happened.

It's all a dream, a fantasy, but that's what I want. I want everything to go back to the way it was, any way that will work. I don't really believe sex is going to do it, but I wouldn't mind trying.

I've waited more than two years now and I'm so close: twenty blocks away from my real home. I don't think I can wait much longer. But I don't want to rush in and ruin everything. I know I'm not just going to wake up, not just like that. I still have to figure out how to undo what's been done.

Unfortunately I don't have much time to think about it right now. I've got so much else to do. I have assignments, seminars to get to, books to buy. I have to call Ava a couple of times a week and tell her I'm all right and make sure she and Avo are managing without me. I email Susan. I talk to Alison when we both get back to res in the afternoons. We've been getting on okay since we bonded over storage containers. Of course she regresses, but whenever she sees me stepping over her shoes, she grabs them and puts them away on her side of the room.

Anyway, I let a week go by before I phone Krystal again.

"Don't call me Krystal," she says.

But I'm not calling her Amy. I'd rather call her Girl.

We arrange to get together on Wednesday afternoon again. This time I set it up so we'll go for a walk. "Bring Wolfie," I tell her. She's okay with that.

I'm excited all week thinking about it. Poor old Wolfie, it's been over two years since I've seen him. And a year and a half since I talked to him on the other side of the door on that awful PD day.

Will he even know me after all this time?

Wednesday comes, and exactly at three thirty I'm waiting outside Starbucks with my coffee. Five minutes later I see them coming along the street, Krystal in shaggy boots, her long black hair swinging —and Wolfie. Wolfie!

I'm shocked at how white he's got around the muzzle. He's eight. My heart is thumping.

"Yo, Wolfie," I call, and he strains forward on his leash. When he's ten feet away he starts shuffling his back end. Next thing I know he's jumping up like he's not supposed to, licking my face.

Krystal shoves the leash into my hand. "I'm gonna go get a coffee."

He knows me. *He knows me!* His big brown eyes glisten and he yips and whines and wriggles frantically. I put my coffee down and stroke his silky ears and scratch the top of his tail the way I always used to. He's in heaven. So am I. He knows me!

I murmur silly things in his ears. "You poor old fat thing, did you miss me? Did you miss your mommy? Of course I came back for you like I promised. Of course I wouldn't ever forget you."

I'm crouching with my arms around him, people skirting

around us on the sidewalk, when Krystal comes out again. And Wolfie leaps out of my arms and runs to her.

"Get down!" she cries.

I watch him waggling his back end around in front of her, whining with excitement. Then he comes back to me. What's going on in that little pea brain? Is he just being friendly to me? Does he really know me at all?

"I think he's confused," says Krystal, picking up his leash.

My coffee's all over the sidewalk. I pick up the cup and throw it away.

"Let's walk to the ravine over by Mount Pleasant," she says and hands me back Wolfie's leash. He doesn't care if there's two of me. He's not letting it bother him. All he's thinking about now is his walk. He's happy.

"I don't want you calling me Krystal," she says. "I'm not talking to you if you do."

"I can see your point. I wouldn't want to be called Krystal either. So I changed my name. Why can't you pick a new one too?"

"I don't want to." She gets this furtive look on her face. "They wouldn't like it. Amy's fine with me."

By "they" I assume she means Mom. But at least she doesn't say it, which is good, because every time she does I want to slap her. "You're not so much of a rebel now, are you?"

She doesn't like that. "It's not the same, is it?" she snaps.

We walk. "You could call me Aimee," she says after a while. "Like in French."

"What's the difference? It sounds just the same."

"Well, fine." Wolfie snuffles at the bottom of trees, at spots on the sidewalk. "What about Emmy?"

"You don't look like an Emmy, not in a million years. But okay," I say grudgingly. "I'll give it a try. Krystal-Emmy. K-Em."

Then I tell Krystal-Emmy about my cottage fantasy, leaving out the part at the end when I turn back into me. I stop at the point where Greg gives me his business card and welcomes me into the firm.

"It ain't gonna happen," she says.

The thing is, I'm not in a position of power here. She could refuse to have anything more to do with me, and what could I do about it? Nothing.

I have to make her *want* to see me. It has to be the two of us against the world. I can't afford to be angry with her. I have to hide how unfair it feels to me that she's taken my home and family, because she didn't do it on purpose. Of course I have her home and family now, even if—except for Ava and Avo—it isn't that great a trade. I have to be nice, not make her uncomfortable, not pressure her about what I want. Because she knows I want something.

The bottom line is I have to stay in touch with her, keep things moving. I can't let her cut me off.

So when I call her on Sunday and leave a message and she doesn't get back to me right away, I can't help panicking. I go through it all over again: Why should she call back? What's in it for her? What have I got that she needs? She has security, a loving home, all the stuff she could want. A glamorous job that pays good money, even if I don't approve of it. All I am to her is danger.

Not that much danger, surely? Who's going to believe me, Mia Marques from nowhere? The only person who might is Mom, if I could make her slow down enough to listen. If she didn't run me over again first, or have me hauled off in a straitjacket before I could say what I had to. I could prove to her that I know things that no one but Amy could know. Certainly not the impostor in my place.

Anyway, next morning K-Em does call back, so the panic's over. We meet at Starbucks again on Wednesday, and she even agrees to get together every week or so. Nowhere near the house, though—she makes it plain she doesn't trust me anywhere around there. I'm not even sure why she says yes to keep on seeing me. She must be getting something out of it. She must be lonely, no matter how nice her life is. I guess I'm a link to familiar things for her, just like she is to me.

"Don't you want to see your grandparents again?" I ask her.

"Not really."

"But they love you. They always loved you."

"Oh yeah?" She tosses her hair over her shoulder with her hand. "They threw me out. First they threw my mom and me out, and then they threw me out again, by myself." Her eyes are hard.

"Only because they were afraid of what might happen to you. They were scared you'd get hurt. Drinking and taking drugs."

"I wasn't taking drugs."

"You would have, sooner or later. I've seen it happen. It couldn't have been easy for them, looking after a kid. They're old, and they didn't understand you. You were so angry, too."

"I had every right to be."

"I know, I know. But they felt bad that they couldn't look after you properly. They were like that with me too. They went all strange on me a couple of times when they thought I'd taken off."

She shrugs. "They just wanted to control me, and they were pissed when they couldn't. They should have loved me enough to keep me, and they didn't."

I let it go. I love Ava and Avo now, and they love me—especially Ava, but Avo does too, in his way. Of course it helps that I'm not drinking or taking drugs or slutting around. It helps that I'm making something of myself, fulfilling their dreams for me.

Chapter 28

Meanwhile, it's not like I've got nothing to do besides tiptoe around Miss Has-It-All. I've got classes. I've got group projects where half the people in the group are lazy slackers and I'm working twice as hard to carry them. I'm used to getting eighties and nineties. "That's going to change," the profs keep telling us. It's not going to change for me.

I don't even like commerce all that much. Most people are in the program because they want to make money. There's a few nice people, a couple of them who want to change the world, make it a better place, but a lot of them are just rich jerks. They want the lifestyle. I admit I don't have a lot of lofty motives myself. I'm in it because I can do it, because I got a scholarship that brought me here.

At least Alison and I are getting on okay. We talk about things, or actually I ask questions and she talks. One night when she's had a bit too much to drink, she complains she's been here almost a month and she hasn't found a boyfriend. She confesses she came to U of T because more guys come here.

"Oh, come on," I say. Okay, maybe some people think that, but they don't go around admitting it. It's not cool.

"It's true," she insists. "A lot of universities, the ratio of girls to guys is sixty–forty. Seventy–thirty in some courses. Who's going to pick me with all that competition? At least the odds are better here."

"Don't be so hard on yourself," I tell her. She's not looking so great at the moment, with her mascara smeared under her eyes and her hair all over the place. "You're really a nice person, Alison. I don't mean you're not attractive, but in the end what guys want is basically somebody who won't give them a hard time."

"Oh, thanks," she snorts. She gives me a fishy look. Who am I to tell her what guys want when I have absolutely no sign of a social life? I don't say that in my old life it used to be different. I had lots of great friends once.

After we turn the lights out, I lie awake and wonder what they're all doing now. I'd give anything to be able to see them. It's weird to be living so close and not to have had any sightings, like walking along Bloor Street. But K-Em says most of the old gang left town for university. Hardly anybody picked U of T. Abby's at Dalhousie and Elly is at some castle in England.

"What about Nate?" I asked her, casually, like he didn't mean any more to me than any of the rest of them.

"Out West, at Simon Fraser."

First I'd heard of it. Then I asked if she had his email and she said yes, but she wouldn't give it to me. She said he'd only emailed her once since he left. I don't know what that means.

If he's that far away, I guess he won't be back for Thanksgiving, but for sure he'll be back at Christmas. I asked her if she'd consider having a party with Nate and everybody there—and inviting me too. Her face closed up right away. She hasn't changed her mind about letting me come anywhere near the house.

I haven't seen anyone I know from Kingston either, although a couple of kids from Regi are here. K-Em asked me that time if I'd heard from Loki. I feel kind of guilty—I haven't called him or anything since we both got here. I meant to call him but I didn't. I try to remember if he was mad at me about anything the last time I saw him. I think we were fairly friendly by then. He was all excited about getting out of Kingston. I wonder how he's getting on with his program. It's the same as ever: If we're going to keep in touch, I'm the one who'll have to make the effort.

I get this idea in my head about bringing him and K-Em together. Exactly what would be the point? I'm not sure. Maybe because he'd be one more link between us. Maybe because there'd be three of us who knew.

Next day I check Facebook and, amazingly, Loki is on it and his number is listed. Even more amazing, he picks up right away. "It's Mia," I say. "Remember me?"

"Took you long enough," he says, but not grumpily. "What do you want?"

We arrange to meet next day at the McDonald's near Yonge and Wellesley. When he walks up to me, I don't even recognize him, except that he's wearing his ratty old Chelsea scarf. The thing is, he's shaved his head. I'm used to seeing him shaking his hair out of his eyes so he can see. Besides, all guys with shaved heads look alike.

He doesn't hug me or anything, but he has this big grin on his face. He points to his shiny skull. "You like it?"

"I'll get used to it. At least your head is a good shape. It's just you don't look like you."

It's also strange seeing him out of context. We're a little part of Kingston's north end on Yonge Street, the centre of the universe.

We decide to get something to eat elsewhere and walk down Yonge Street. Loki seems taller than he used to be, and for the first time I've known him he isn't wearing droopy-ass pants and a hoodie. He's actually in regular guy clothes, normal-sized jeans and quite a nice black leather jacket. He looks almost cool. That jacket must have made a hole in his OSAP loan.

He loves Toronto—he's got a place out on the Danforth. He loves his film program. He's even working at some student radio station as a DJ, which is not bad for a guy who when I first got to know him would hardly say two words in public. He's helping somebody make a film.

I make the mistake of asking him what it's about.

"There's this guy, see," he says, "and he finds this like, three-foot iguana in a parking lot in the middle of February." And he's off. We amble along the busy street while he tells me this long, involved plot. It's just like the old days. I love it that he still gets so excited. I was afraid he might have grown out of it.

We find a little pita place and when we're eating he actually asks me how I like my courses. He never would have done that in the old days. I tell him about my classes and living in residence. Neither of us mentions K-Em.

When I meet her the next day, I tell her I saw him. She acts like, whatever, but she's listening. "He looks amazing," I tell her. "He's shaved his head because he said he wasn't projecting the right image. Can you imagine that? Loki? He's already got some radio job."

"I didn't think he'd get off his skateboard long enough to finish high school." She looks down into her coffee cup and mutters something.

"What?"

"I said, not that I have. Finished school."

I try to make her feel better. "You've had a lot to deal with. You'll do it, when you need to. Anyway, next time Loki and I get together, you have to come."

"Why would I want to do that?" She looks alarmed.

"Well, you know—I had the idea you two were pretty good friends."

"That was a long time ago."

I don't know why I'm so set on getting them together. Maybe

I just want to see what happens, how they react. When I bring the idea up with Loki, there's a long silence at the other end of the phone. "Uh-uh," he finally says.

"But you used to like her."

"Krystal. I liked Krystal."

"She's still Krystal inside."

"It's too crazy. I wouldn't know what to say to her."

"Pretend it's a movie. *Freaky Friday*, remember? *The Shaggy DA*."

"It's not a movie."

It takes weeks of hard work. Finally I get them both in the same place, a café over on the Danforth near where he lives. He's already there when we come in. He sees me first and then her. He gets up, and I can see his eyes widen. I mean, he doesn't know her, this tall slender girl with the dark hair and haunted eyes.

But she knows him. She's walking slowly toward him, trying to smile, but her face crumples. When she gets up to him, she throws her arms around his neck and starts to cry. She cries and cries.

It's like there's nobody else in the room but them, like I'm not even there. Awkwardly, he pats her shoulder. "It's okay," he says. "It's okay."

Chapter 29

I wake up from a dream, my heart pounding. It's so real and vivid that at first I don't know where I am. I'm sure I'm at the lake and then gradually I realize I'm in my dorm room, an arm's length from my sleeping roommate. The sense of loss is so overpowering I want to howl.

In the dream I'm at the quarry, on the highest ledge, and the sun is shining. The rock is warm under the soles of my feet. A hawk is circling way up above, watching, waiting. It's waiting for me to jump—me and K-Em. Because it's both of us there, standing at the edge of the rock, which seems like it's hundreds of feet above the water, not like it is in real life. And the other thing that's strange is the deep blue mountains on the horizon. It's like pictures I've seen of the Grand Canyon, or Middle Earth.

I'm not the least bit afraid about jumping. I'm excited and absolutely sure this is what I'm meant to do. I wave to the hawk, like a signal, and he tips a wing like he's giving me the okay. K-Em and I step off together into space. We don't fall straight down, though— we float gently down on the wind. It's a controlled descent. And I'm filled with joy, because when we land, it'll be over. I'll be back to me again.

But I'm awake, and I'm not me. I'm still Mia.

My heart is going a mile a minute. I lie there for a long time listening to it thud. I try to get back into the warm, happy dream space, to go back to that warm, sunny ledge, but I'm too awake. And too grief-stricken that none of it was real.

It's still so incredibly clear in my mind. I can still see every ripple in the lake, feel the wind rushing past us on the way down. And the thing is, I hardly ever dream—not just since the accident, but ever. I used to get so mad at the breakfast table when Mom and Meaghan told each other their dreams, and I never had any to tell. Or if I did dream, it was gone by the time I got out of bed.

This dream is different. Is there something it's trying to tell me? Is that really what dreams do? I lie there and ponder what it could be. It seems like hours go by, and it's still only 4 a.m. Finally I crawl out of bed so I won't wake Alison, and go into the bathroom to do the only thing I can think of: I start work on my next commerce paper.

But all day long the dream sticks with me. I've stopped feeling the sadness that it wasn't real. I hang on to the glorious happiness of it and it casts a glow over everything. I keep having the impulse to call K-Em and tell her, like the dream is some piece of news I've had. I squash that impulse firmly. I know it's not any news that she wants to hear.

Except for one week when she went to New York for some modelling thing, I've seen her every Wednesday. We're talking more easily now about how our lives used to be. But she doesn't like it when I try to move the discussion to what we can do about our future. Her future's fine, she lets me know. My future's my own problem to solve. K-Em has a secretive side. I've got a hunch she's been in touch with Loki at least once since I set it up for them to meet, but she doesn't tell me anything. I'd really like to know what they talk about.

I also keep wondering if she's heard any more from Nate. Suddenly she's cagey about it. "Why do you keep asking?" she frowns.

"Why do you think?"

We're having a sandwich at a place near Yonge and Bloor on one of our weekly "dates." She bites into a huge chicken-mango wrap with mayo. She's not worrying about gaining weight. I know—that metabolism used to be mine. I'm having a salad.

"You mean there was stuff between you?" she says. "It didn't seem like there was a lot."

She doesn't say it in a mean way, but I flare up. "And there was more between you and him?"

She chews her mouthful deliberately and swallows. "Well, something, anyway. You don't have to snap at me."

"I'm sorry. But we liked each other, okay? It hadn't gone very far, but it would have. He called after the accident. I know he cared."

"Makes sense," she concedes. "He hung around a lot at the hospital, and then when I went home he came to the house. But it was really awkward. I didn't know what I was supposed to say to him. I didn't know how things were, like, before, and I couldn't very well ask him. I liked him, but it was still, well, awkward. I know he felt bad it didn't work out."

Not as bad as I'd feel if it had. "So have you heard from him lately?"

"A bit."

"Is he still coming back for Christmas?"

"As far as I know."

It's like pulling teeth. "Will you set something up so I can see him? *Please?*"

She frowns. "He'll think I want to start things up again."

"Just get the three of us together for coffee. Or a beer. I'll make sure he doesn't get the wrong message."

She puts down her wrap and looks me in the eye. "Do you think that's such a good idea, Mia?"

"*Yes.* I do."

"I mean, think about it. What about him?"

"What do you mean, him?"

"Like, think of how he's got to feel. I mean, we can't *tell* him."

"It's just a coffee, okay?"

"Okay, okay," she says. "I'll try."

I don't believe her.

Then one cold, windy November afternoon she and I are walking along Bloor when somebody calls out, "Hey, Ame!" Both of us turn. A tall, lean guy in a leather jacket with dark hair is hurrying towards us. All of a sudden I can't breathe.

"Nate!" K-Em gives me a quick look. "I can't believe it. What are you doing back here?"

His face goes solemn. "Family stuff. My grandfather's funeral."

"Omigod, Nate."

"That's awful," I say, thinking of Avo.

"Thanks." He glances at me quickly, then back to her. "It's sad. But he'd been sick for a long time. We were expecting it."

He isn't really seeing me—he's too dazzled by her. She looks almost Japanese, her face pale in the cold wind, the dead-straight glossy black hair, the kohl-rimmed eyes. "I can't get over how different you look," he says.

"Yeah, well. Oh, this is Mia."

He tears his eyes away from her again long enough to say "Hi."

"Mia's got a four-year scholarship at U of T," she tells him.

"Cool. What are you taking?" This time he looks right at me, for three seconds.

Can't you see me, Nate?

"Commerce." It comes out in a sort of squeak. I clear my throat and say, louder, "What are you doing at Simon Fraser?"

"Economics."

"Hey, what a coincidence, you guys," says K-Em. "Almost the same thing."

"Well, no," I say.

"Not exactly," he says at the same time. He smiles at her.

"I wanted to do economics," I say. "Or development studies. Now I wish I had."

"You're in first year, right? Plenty of time to switch." He shifts from one foot to another, hands in his pockets.

The wind blows my hair around. I'm shivering. I'm just about to ask if we can go in somewhere warm for coffee when he says, "Guess I better get moving."

I nudge K-Em, hard, and she says to him, "You going to come home again for the Christmas break?"

"Yeah, sure. I'll let you know when I get back out West." They hug goodbye, and Nate says politely to me, "Nice to meet you." Doesn't say my name, obviously doesn't remember it. I watch him walk away down the dark street and turn the corner. I feel like a door is shutting on my heart.

K-Em is saying something to me. I don't even hear her the first time.

She repeats it. "Did you have to make me feel stupid like that?"

"Like what?" I turn to look at her in surprise. "What are you talking about?"

"Like I didn't know the difference between economics and commerce. Like I was so stupid I thought they were the same."

"Well, they're not, but no big deal."

"You didn't have to *laugh* at me."

What's she going on about? I push the image of Nate disappearing down the street out of my mind. "I didn't laugh. Or if I did, it was only because I was nervous."

She starts walking fast down the street. I have to trot after her to keep up. "Sorry. You don't have to worry about Nate thinking you're stupid. He thinks you're a goddess."

"Hardly."

Which just goes to show how someone can look absolutely gorgeous and still have no self-confidence at all. Not that it helps me any.

Chapter 30

At the end of November, exam countdown starts. First one down, four to go. Three, two, one, and I'm done.

I promised Ava that as soon I was finished, I'd head back home for Christmas. The afternoon after my last exam I grab my bags and rush to catch the Kingston bus, falling into a seat just as the doors close. I'm a wreck from weeks of non-stop studying, but I think I did well enough to hold onto my scholarship.

I'm excited to be seeing Ava and Avo again, but I wish I knew what was going on with K-Em. I won't see her now for nearly three weeks. I never got a chance to say goodbye. I called before I left, but she was out. She called back and left a message that she was sorry we hadn't managed to get together, but she didn't say I should call her back. Will she miss me? Or will she be relieved to have me out of her life for a while?

Less than a week to go before Christmas, and it's a letdown that there's no snow when we roll into Kingston. But every house is lit with coloured lights, and snow or not, I'm getting into the holiday spirit. I splurge on a cab, and ten minutes later I'm standing in front of Ava and Avo's place on James Street. It feels like I've been away for ages.

Ava comes to the door before I can get out my key. I'm shocked at how she seems to have shrunk and got a lot older. She makes little excited cries when she sees it's me. Her eyes look teary, but her false teeth gleam from ear to ear. "So beautiful you look!" She wipes her hands on her apron and tries to wrestle my bags out of my hands. "So fancy!"

I'm wearing a new black quilted jacket and my famous, fabulous Spanish boots. I tower over her. "Ava, leave my bags alone! They're too heavy for you." We struggle over them and I manage to make her drop them so I can hug her.

She's scrubbed and polished every inch of my old room. Jesus and Mary beam down from their usual places on the wall, and I give them each a big smile back. "Come, come," Ava says, as soon as I get my coat off, and leads me to the living room. "I show you."

Standing in front of the window is a Christmas tree.

It's a scotch pine, quite a big one. The box of ornaments is out, waiting for me to hang them.

She beams, delighted at my astonishment. "Your Avo, he ask his friend to bring one from the country. Nice fresh tree, not a supermarket one."

In the kitchen the counters are crowded with Ava's baking. "To feed you up. You are much too skinny." She pinches my cheek. "More meat on a butcher's knife than on those bones! No wonder you have no boyfriend."

"I'm not too thin," I protest. I've stayed the same weight for over a year. "I ate all the cookies you sent me. Well, my roommate ate half. You'll have to teach me to make them." She looks pleased. I never showed much interest in cooking, just in healthy food.

Avo comes in from somewhere just in time for supper. He's looking older too. "What a beautiful tree, Avo," I say. "What a wonderful surprise." I hug him, although he doesn't hug easily. He feels kind of like wood, but he kisses me on each cheek and smiles.

When we sit down to eat together, he says his usual grace:

"Our holy Father bless this food. Bless our daughter and keep her in your care." By that he means Krystal's mother, and he must be grateful to leave her in God's care. "Our holy Father thank you for bringing our dear girl home." This time he means me. Ava seconds his amen, and so do I.

After he finishes his meal, he takes his mug of tea down to the basement. As Ava and I do the dishes, I hear him hammering away. "What's he doing, Ava?" I ask. "I'm going down to see."

"No, no, not allowed," she says, firmly taking my arm. "You stay here and fix the tree."

That night, in my old bed—no plastic over the mattress anymore, that's long gone—I think over how things have worked out in Toronto. Not bad in some ways. I've connected with K-Em, and that's a big hurdle passed. Even though she still doesn't trust me, she acknowledges that we're linked. We're wary, but we're getting to know each other. I mustn't be impatient. It's only the start.

But I wish she'd said goodbye before I left. And why didn't she arrange something with Nate, like she said she would? I want to trust her but it's hard. I can't help feeling she still wants him for herself.

I don't have much Christmas shopping to do, as I did most of it in Toronto. I've brought some textbooks for my next term's courses to get a head start. Ava clucks her tongue when I set them on my desk. "You must have a holiday," she protests. "You make yourself sick with all this study, study, study! You are young. You must have some fun."

When I first came to live here, they were worried I'd have too much fun. I hardly know how to start, but I try. I make a date to go to Tiffin's for breakfast with my rowing team. I go to visit my friend Shelley. She loves the social work program she's in. It's great sitting on the big couch with her and her little sister again, watching DVDs and eating popcorn with a bunch of cats and dogs on our laps.

Susan calls and makes a date for lunch. The night before, I actually hunt up that old book she lent me two years ago, about Valancy and her horrible family. I read until two in the morning. I finally really get into it. Especially the part about the poor little plain girl always comparing herself to her perfect, golden-haired cousin.

I glue the falling-out pages back into the book, and at lunch I give it back to Susan. "I know why you gave it to me," I say. "Valancy has to get over feeling stuck and trapped. She has to take charge of her life. She has to kill her old self, which was a lie anyway, and take risks. The idea of death sets her free."

Susan looks a little uneasy. "I don't think I expected it to spur you to action after reading it. I was afraid you'd find it silly, but it's always been one of my never-fail escapes. Whenever I find myself feeling stuck or sorry for myself, I pick it up. I think it's one of the most honest things Montgomery ever did. She really lets the hypocrites of this world have it, and there were a lot of them in her world, I'm afraid." She smiles at me. "So how are you, Mia? You look wonderful."

"I'm okay. You look wonderful too."

She does, actually. Her hair is shorter and less grey. But she looks older too, like Ava and Avo.

She wants to know all about U of T, even though I've been emailing her regularly. I tell her some more about my classes and my roommate. She laughs when I tell her I've taught Alison to be organized. "And the poor girl didn't request to be moved?"

"No. I can compromise, you know. But I didn't have to."

She doesn't ask about K-Em, although I told her we've been in touch. Susan has never believed in encouraging me in my *delusion*. "I'm telling you anyway," I say. "You're not my social worker, remember? You're my friend."

"I know."

I tell her about meeting K-Em in Starbucks, how incredible it felt to see her for the first time. I tell about how hard I've worked to get her to trust me.

After a while Susan starts to ask questions. "Why has she gone along with all of this? I get the feeling you wanted the relationship more than she did. What does she get out of it?"

"I don't know, exactly," I admit. "It's like we're related, sort of like sisters. You could say we share the same DNA—just not at the same time."

"Have you been to the house?"

"No. She won't let me near it."

"And why do you think that is?"

"Because she doesn't trust me not to make a horrible scene in front of my mother? Because she's protecting her, and herself? I can live with that. I'll show her she can trust me."

Susan nods thoughtfully.

"You haven't told anybody about this, have you?" I ask.

"Of course not."

"It's not a secret." But it is, really. One that everyone who knows it is helping me keep.

On Christmas Eve I go to bed with flutters in my stomach, like when I was a kid. But I feel sad too. Christmas is the time I miss my family most, miss Mom and my dad, miss Meaghan. When I was little, the pesky little kid sister, it was the one night I was allowed to sleep in Meaghan's room. I wanted to be sure we'd get up at the same time if Santa came. So she wouldn't get more presents than me.

I jolt awake at 3 a.m. dreaming again about the quarry. I lie there until the feelings ebb—the rush of joy, the sadness of waking and knowing it's only a dream. I've had it at least three times now. I don't feel so destroyed anymore when I wake up and find I'm still Mia. Even in the dream I've sort of started to know I'm dreaming, and I jump off that cliff every time just the same. Does it mean anything? It has to mean something. Am I getting closer? Is that how it's really going to end?

I get up to get a glass of water from the kitchen, and as I walk past the living room, I stop and look at the ornaments on the tree, glinting in the light from the street. In front of the tree I make out a bulky shape that wasn't there when I went to bed. It must be what Avo has been working on in the basement.

There's just enough light so I can read the label on it: *To Krystiana Maria from her Avo.* I go back to bed feeling comforted and lucky after all.

When I wake next, the sun is shining and I smell baking. Ava is making her Christmas rolls. I got her red sheepskin-lined slippers to replace her shabby old ones, and she puts them on and to my relief they fit perfectly. Avo unwraps the big book on Portugal I bought him and shows me pictures of Porto, near where he was born. It looks magical, like something out of a fairy tale, like Valancy's blue castles.

Ava's knitted me a lovely sweater, soft dark-blue wool, with a hood. My gift from Avo turns out to be a big chest, carved and painted with a country scene. He has painted one side with a summer scene, winter on the other, so I can turn one side out or the other, depending on the season. It has little houses and horses and angels in a bright blue sky.

He watches my face. "I make it of cedar," he says. "To keep out moths."

I'm stunned. "It's beautiful, Avo. Amazing." The hours he must have put into it! "I never knew you could make anything like this. And you painted it too!"

"A hope chest," says Ava slyly. "For when you marry."

"You'll have to wait a long time for that. I'll use it while you're waiting." I run my fingers over the carving on the top. "Avo, it's the most wonderful thing anyone's ever given to me." And it's true. He lets me hug him again, twice in five days.

I don't tell them I doubt I'll ever get married. How could I live my life with someone and not tell the truth about what's happened? And who'd believe me? I don't think it'd be a good idea for me to have kids, either. For all I know, my DNA could have got scrambled in the switch. I'd probably have two-headed babies.

I go to mass with them and we come home and eat a huge meal: potato dumpling soup, rice and salt cod salad, turkey. Afterwards I think I'll die unless I get out for a walk. I call Loki. I know he's home.

"I'll be there in ten," he says.

Ava makes a fuss over him and rubs her hand over his shaved head. "So smooth and shiny! What a man you are! No more little Raymond." She fills a bag for him with chocolate tarts, almond biscuits, and sugar doughnuts.

We head down to the river. There's no ice on the bay yet, and the ducks and geese are still hanging around the rowing docks. We go and sit down out on the end, swinging our legs above the water. "How's it going?" I ask him. He doesn't seem very cheerful.

"Shitty."

"Tell me." I hope his misery doesn't have anything to do with K-Em.

"Aw, nothing new. Just my usual asshole brother thinks I'm full of myself because I got out and he didn't. He keeps trying to get me to take a swing at him so he can pound me to a pulp. It's not like I'm mouthing off or anything. I don't know if I'll ever get a job out of Ryerson, but at least I'm trying. Not like him." He lets out a deep breath. "When you going back?"

"After New Years."

"I'm going before. I don't need to hang around and take any more crap. Anyway, there's a movie opening in Toronto I want to see. K-Em wants to see it too."

She does, does she? "You've been talking to her?"

"Yeah."

"She didn't call *me*." I look over at him and he's smiling a bit. I hope she doesn't break his heart.

When I get back in, Ava is still in the kitchen. "The kettle is hot. I make you tea." We finished Christmas dinner two hours ago and I didn't think I'd ever be hungry again, but when she sets out a plate of her almond tarts, I take one. "Good for you," she nods.

She hands me an oval from a Kleenex box with her spidery writing on it. "I take a message while you were gone. Nice girl but with a funny name. Calling from Toronto."

And I see she's written "KM," and the familiar number.

Chapter 31

"You call her back." She points to the phone.

"It's long distance, Ava." Scandalous.

"It's only money."

K-Em picks up right away. "I though it'd be you. You left without saying goodbye, you rat."

"I thought that was how you wanted it. I figured you were busy."

"Don't be like that, Mia. So Merry Christmas." She lowers her voice, as if Ava is listening. "I talked to my grandmother. Incredible. Of course, she didn't know it was me."

That's because you've got my voice. I don't say it. Ava *is* listening.

"When are you coming back?" K-Em asks. "I'm having a party."

And she's inviting me?

"Not New Years Eve, but the night after," she goes on. "Before everybody heads back to school."

"Where?"

"At the house."

"You'd let me come to the house?" I can't believe it. My heart begins to race. "Who's going to be there?"

"Not a lot of people. Nobody's let me know for sure yet. Just some of the old crowd. Are you okay with that?"

I don't know, but she's letting me into the house. That's major. And letting me see my old friends. Will I see Mom too?

I take a deep breath. "What about Nate? Is he coming?"

"I don't think so. Sorry. He says his flight out is booked for three days from now. Sorry, Mia," she repeats. "I tried."

"Have you seen him?"

"We've just talked on the phone. But I probably will, before he goes."

When I put the phone down, Ava is watching at me.

"I've been invited to a party." My voice wobbles a little. "In Toronto."

She's all smiles. "Nice girl. And who is this 'Nate'? A boyfriend, maybe?"

"No, Ava. He's my friend's boyfriend."

"Ah, too bad."

Yeah, it is.

Loki calls me fifteen minutes later. "Did she invite you?"

So she's called him *again*. "You're going to the party? We can go together."

"Aw, I don't know if I'm gonna go. I won't know anybody. Bunch of rich snobs."

"Don't worry, I'll introduce you. I'll know everybody." It's just that they won't know me. "So what's going on with you and K-Em?"

Silence.

"Okay, I get it. It's private, right?"

"Yeah."

"Well, be careful you don't get hurt."

"Huh," he says. Next day he leaves for Toronto, and I go around to Shelley's house and hang out some more. Her cute brother Jason is home from forest rangers' college. I get invited to dinner, and Shelley, Jason, Cayley, and I make a huge spaghetti for the whole family. Jason flirts with me while we chop vegetables. Everybody jokes around and teases each other at dinner. It's a normal family. "You can come over and cook any time," Shelley's dad says to me.

It's all great, but part of me can't stop worrying about getting back to Toronto. I've hardly been able to sleep since K-Em called. I'm terrified a blizzard or an ice storm or some other natural disaster is going to stop me from getting there for the day after New Years. I'll get there if I have to walk.

The weather stays good, and there's no problem getting back. The bus isn't even crowded. All I can think about now is seeing Mom. What will I say to her? I have a horrible thought—what if she doesn't like me? She used to take against my friends sometimes for no reason I could see. Elly was "too pushy," and Gabby was "a real little madam." What's she going to think about me?

I've put a lot of time into trying to decide what to wear. If I was still Amy, I'd hardly give it a thought. Just something that would show my toned butt and abs but not too much skin. I was never into display much, until the time I decided to jump off a cliff to impress Nate Dubinsky.

But now that I'm Mia, it takes more dressing up to look okay. After getting every skirt and top I own out of my closet and trying them on, in the end I decide on casual: good black jeans, medium-heel boots, and a skinny top.

Loki meets me in the subway at Bloor and Yonge and we go the last three stops together. As we walk the four blocks to the house, a few flakes of snow tumble out of the sky. I'm so nervous I don't notice at first that Loki knows the way.

"You've been there already!"

"So?"

"You didn't tell me. I bet you met Wolfie too."

"Her dog? Yeah."

The house is lit with about a million Christmas lights. I wonder if that Greg guy is putting them up these days. There's more snow than in Kingston, but the walks are neatly shovelled. "She says the back door's open," Loki says. "The party's upstairs, up in her room."

By the time we get there I'm having trouble breathing. He pushes open the door and I follow him in. I'm quaking. At any second I could run into Mom.

But the door into the main part of the house is shut. I stop and listen, but all is quiet in there. I don't even hear Wolfie. Music and laughter float down from the third floor. "This way," says Loki impatiently. I give up staring at the closed door and follow him up the two flights to the top. To my old room.

It's hard to get my bearings in the dimness. The only illumination is strings of coloured Christmas tree lights. My bed is gone, replaced by a futon. The space doesn't even seem the same shape —it feels bigger somehow. There are lots of chairs and sofas that weren't there before, and a new breakfast bar with a little fridge and sink.

Slowly my eyes get accustomed to the light. I count fifteen people. And spot Gabby and Elly, Damian and Ted. No Nate, of course—like K-Em said, he'll be back out West by now.

"Loki! Mia!" K-Em waves from behind the counter. She's wearing a shiny little black dress with red tights. Her hair with its Chinese bangs is so straight, it looks like a wig. She leans over and gives us both Toronto kisses, lips smacking the air by our cheeks. "Mom's not here," she says quickly. "She's at Greg's, so we can make as much noise as we like. As long as the police don't come."

"Where's Wolfie?" I ask. "I didn't hear him bark."

"He was barking lots earlier. He probably got bored and went to sleep."

She opens some vodka coolers for us and then drags us over to the group in the corner. "Hey, everybody," she cries, "you have to meet my friend Mia. She's from Kingston, like Loki."

They all look so different to me, but it's been two and a half years, what do I expect? Gabby's cut her hair off short and bleached it platinum. Elly is wearing makeup, but other than that, she looks the same. Gabby jumps up and hugs Loki, so I guess they've met before. "So you two know each other from Kingston?" she asks me.

"Loki and I go a long way back," I say.

"Mia's in commerce at U of T," says K-Em. "That's right, isn't it, Mia, commerce?"

"At the moment."

"She's so smart. She's got a big scholarship."

I'm embarrassed. It's not the kind of thing I would ever have said, but nobody seems to notice.

As new people come in, K-Em keeps jumping up to welcome them. I notice that Loki's helping her, taking coats and mopping up when somebody knocks over a glass. I notice that he's acting like her boyfriend.

It isn't a noisy party. Everybody obviously just wants to sit around and get caught up. Ted's just come back from a year in Japan, and he's telling a long, involved story about ordering puffer fish in a fancy restaurant in Tokyo. Apparently it's supposed to be some kind of amazing delicacy. "Also very expensive," he says, "because it has to be cooked properly or it's poisonous. But everybody said we had to try it, so we decided to order one and split it between five of us. The problem was the waiter didn't understand and brought us five of them. The bill came to six hundred dollars."

Everybody shrieks.

"Did you pay it?"

"We had to. We didn't want to cause an international incident. I starved for the rest of the month."

"How did it taste?" Damian asks.

"Expensive."

Jenn comes in and everybody hugs her. People talk about the plays we all had parts in during high school and the soccer games we used to play using our own special rules. And rowing—Elly and Ted and Damian still row. Everyone is being silly and goofy. Any minute somebody is going to start on the Monty Python Dead Parrot sketch. Sitting there watching, I'm feeling like a ghost.

Jenn touches my arm. "Sorry about this. It must be awfully boring for you to listen to. It's rude of us, really."

"I don't mind," I protest. "It reminds me of my old school."

She tells me she's taking philosophy at U of T, and we compare our course loads. "Amy says you're a rower too," she says.

"I coxed for the club in Kingston. I haven't even tried to row at U of T."

"I'm still hanging on with my old club. But, yeah, forget it at U of T. The Branksome Hall girls have got it sewn up. I wouldn't have picked you out as a rower, though."

"I'm out of shape."

"I didn't mean that. You don't look out of shape. I just meant you don't look like a jock. More sophisticated."

This sophisticate has another drink.

After hardly an hour I've had several drinks and my head is throbbing from the strain. Suddenly I just want to get out of there and process everything. I slip past K-Em and out the door with the idea of calling a cab downstairs where it's quiet. I'm unsteady on my feet so I hold tight to the banister, taking the steps very carefully, one at a time.

The bottom door opens and a couple of guys start up. As I open the second floor door and stumble in, one guy calls out, "You okay?"

"Yeah, thanks." I rush for the bathroom. At least I hit the toilet —there's only liquid in my stomach. I sit on the floor until I feel steady enough to get up and wash my face. A sad-faced raccoon stares back from the mirror. My eye makeup is seeping down my cheeks. There's mouthwash in the medicine cabinet and I chug it from the bottle.

I hear a noise behind me and turn in alarm. Wolfie is in the doorway. He's just looking up at me, his head on one side. His tail wags gently.

"Oh, boy." I kneel and hug him. He wriggles and tries to lick my hot face. "What am I going to do, darling?" His big brown eyes are full of concern, but he doesn't have any answers.

A door opens down the hall and brisk footsteps approach. It's K-Em, and she's not happy with me. "What the hell are you doing down here? I thought you'd gone without saying goodbye. I told you Mom wasn't home."

"I wasn't looking for her," I protest. "I wasn't snooping. I'm not doing anything. I just came down to call a cab."

"Well, you can't go now," she snaps. "Nate's here. He and Kevin just arrived."

Chapter 32

Nate! Was that him coming up the stairs? "But—I thought—you said he went back out West."

"He had to change his ticket or something." She looks me over in exasperation. "There's vomit on your top." She's steering me back to the sink, swabbing me with a facecloth. "For God's sake, Mia. I thought you didn't drink."

"I don't. That's the problem."

Loki appears behind her. "She's drunk," K-Em tells him.

I hiccup. "I am not drunk," I say with dignity. "I had two vodka coolers on an empty stomach. It's very stressful for me, being here, okay?"

"Then you know how I've felt for two years."

They march me back upstairs between them. My legs wouldn't hold me up otherwise. Nate is perched on the back of a sofa beside Elly. Out of sheer terror I stick next to Loki by the bar.

"Get over there," K-Em hisses at me. "You said you wanted to see everybody." She puts her arm around my waist and propels me over to the group. "I caught Mia trying to sneak out."

Everybody protests. "Come and sit here," Damian orders. "We'll try and be less boring." He and Jenn shift apart on the sofa to make room. "Have you met Kevin and Nate?"

I never did know Kevin very well. Nate raises a hand and my heart does a big flop.

"You know Mia, Nate," says K-Em. "Remember you ran into us on Bloor when you were back for your grandfather's funeral?"

"Yeah, sure," he says. "Hi, Mia."

Oh, why did I drink so much?

His hair is shorter now, the wild head of curls tamed down. He looks cooler, more adult, but I liked the way he looked before. He's on the far side of Elly so I can't even see him without leaning around her. They're all talking about global warming and arguing Canada's position on the Kyoto Accord.

K-Em puts on a disco CD and turns it up loud. People groan. "The Dancing Queen is at it again," says Ted.

"Come on," orders K-Em, hands on her hips, a jet-haired, red-legged Pippy Longstockings—how can they resist her? "You're a bunch of boring old sticks. Have you already forgotten how to have a good time?"

Loki comes over and pulls me to my feet. "She says we have to dance."

"I didn't know you could dance." I never saw him do it before. He's jerking his head and bobbing like a chicken. I blink at him in amazement. "What on earth is that you're doing?"

"Something I made up."

I dance, acutely conscious of how ridiculous we must look. Jenn and Gabby and Damian join us. K-Em walks over to Nate. He's smiling at her, shaking his head, and then they're dancing too.

I watch them out of the corner of my eye as Loki weaves and bobs. He's making me so dizzy I'm afraid I'll be sick again. Suddenly K-Em lunges forward and Nate takes a step back—into me. I crash to the floor, bringing Loki down with me.

Complete and utter humiliation. The others lean over us,

dragging me up. Nate looks stricken. "Hell, I'm really, really sorry," he says.

"It was my fault," says K-Em. "I'm so clumsy. You okay, Mia?"

"Fine."

"But I've hurt you," Nate says wretchedly. "You're limping."

"That's nothing new. I limp."

"She had a bad accident same time as me," K-Em tells him. "We were in the same hospital. Get the poor girl a drink, you big oaf."

"No! I've already had too much." I'm trying hard not to slur my words. He'll think I fell because I'm a lush.

He heads obediently over to the bar. I limp after him.

"There's gotta be water here somewhere." He finds a bottle in the bar fridge and fills a glass for me. My skin tingles as our fingers brush. "I'm really sorry," he says again. "You sure you're okay?"

I swallow and nod. "I'm fine."

His eyes are on K-Em. "You guys met in the hospital? Funny, I don't remember you. I went to see her a lot there."

"They moved me to another hospital after a few days. She and I only connected again since I came here for university."

"And she remembered you from then? She was really out of it at the beginning."

I'm trying to think of something to cover it that isn't exactly a lie, but I see he's already forgotten what we've been talking about. K-Em and Loki are bobbing and pecking together, and Nate is watching them. "Who's the guy?"

"A friend of mine from Kingston. He's at Ryerson. He and K-Em are friends too."

"I can see that." He doesn't look too happy about it. "You mean Amy, right? Why do you call her K-Em?"

Whoops. Because I'm drunk, but I don't say that. "Sort of a private joke." I nod my head at her and Loki. "Is that okay with you?"

"You mean—" He watches them for a while and shrugs. "Sure,

why not?" And doesn't say anything else.

The song ends and K-Em comes over to where we're standing. "How are you two doing?"

You two. That's pushing it. I look over at Nate, but I don't think it's registered. He's smiling at her.

"I'm fine," I say, like for the third time in five minutes.

"I should head out," Nate says. "I told you I could only stay a couple of minutes." He calls over to Kevin. "You ready to leave, man?"

Kevin isn't quite ready—reprieve. We rejoin the group on the couch. Nate's arm is over the back, behind my head. I can feel the heat of his body. I slip into a kind of trance.

Then he's checking his watch again and saying this time he really has to leave. He's firm. "I gotta be at the airport tomorrow morning at six." Kevin says he'll get a ride with someone else. Nate shrugs his coat on and everybody hugs him goodbye. He and K-Em hold their clinch a moment longer than absolutely necessary. I wonder when and if I'll ever see him again.

And then she whispers something to him, and he comes over to me. "Mia, do you want a lift back to your dorm?"

She's told him to ask me, and he's following orders. "Don't worry about me. I'll call a cab."

"Hey, I just had one beer. It's my dad's car. I'm perfectly sober to drive."

K-Em is already holding my jacket.

On the way downstairs he says, "You're still limping. You are hurt. I feel terrible about falling over you."

"It wasn't your fault. I limp when I'm tired. I'll be back to normal by tomorrow."

I wish.

We walk a block to his car. I step very carefully on the icy sidewalk, wishing I dared to take his arm. The stars are out, but I can't see the moon. The parked cars glisten with frost. Nate opens the passenger door and hangs onto my elbow until I'm safely in. As he puts the key in the ignition, music blares. He turns it down and we sit and wait for the windshield to defrost. Our breath mingles in the space. I try to think of something to say, anything. "What time will you have to get up to go to the airport?" I ask. Brilliant.

"Four, probably. I should just stay up all night, sleep on the plane."

My residence is hardly ten minutes away. "How do you like it out West?" I ask.

"Great," he says politely.

"A big change of scenery, I guess, with the mountains. Not so cold as here, though." And why exactly am I giving this travelogue? "Thanks a lot for the lift," I say as he pulls up at the curb.

"No hard feelings for knocking you over?"

"Of course not. It wasn't anybody's fault. It was great to meet you." Can I get any more inane? Yes: "Have a safe trip," I babble. In an extremity of desperation and hopelessness, I lean over and kiss him, just missing his mouth.

His eyes widen. He starts to say something and then he reaches across to the glove compartment and takes out a pen. "Here's my email," he says, scribbling on a parking lot receipt. "Let me know how that leg is, okay?"

"Okay," I say stupidly.

And then I'm out of the car on the sidewalk like Cinderella, nothing left of the night but the note I clutch in my hand. His tail lights vanish up the street.

When I get up to my room—Alison isn't back from Orillia—I sit on the bed holding the piece of paper for a long time. I even sniff it—pathetic—but I can't detect any scent of Nate. I prop it on my desk beside Ava and Avo's wedding picture. I don't shower, don't even brush my teeth, just get undressed and climb into bed. I can still feel the curve of the corner of his lips. I'm glad I did it, no matter what he thought.

But the adrenalin starts to ebb and I don't feel quite as sure about it. I'm thinking more clearly and feeling very sad. I'm getting what K-Em has been saying all along: He's a nice, decent guy and it isn't fair to him to drag him into this. I won't be emailing him. I just wanted to see him again, and I did. And now that I've got closure, I can move on.

Chapter 33

Alison comes back on Sunday night, full of the great time she's had seeing all her old pals. First thing she does is make a long phone call to Orillia. She's fallen for some guy from her old high school—after all that about coming to U of T to find a man.

"What about you?" she asks. "How was your holiday?"

It was good, I tell her. "I mostly hung out with my grandparents and got caught up with people. I even went to a party."

"You're kidding!" She makes a big deal of my monk-like existence. "I can't believe you went to a party! Aren't you afraid your marks will go to hell?"

"Don't worry, I won't be making a habit of it."

"Did you meet anybody?" She gives me a meaningful look.

"Just old friends from high school."

I don't see K-Em for nearly two weeks. She's away doing a catalogue shoot on some Caribbean island. I've got my glamorous life going to class. When she gets back and gives me a call, almost the first thing she asks is, "Did you hear from Nate?"

"No."

"Huh. That's funny. He was asking about you, so I gave him your email."

"You shouldn't have."

"Why not? I thought you'd be thrilled, you think he's so hot."

"Not any more," I say firmly. "That's over. Anyway, he gave me his email himself. I could have written to him if I wanted to."

"And you didn't? I never understand you, Mia."

"You're the one who didn't want me to see him, back in the fall."

"Yeah, true," she admits. "But I started thinking it was kind of mean of me to want to control it."

"No, you were right the first time. It's not fair to get him involved again. It's not like it can go anywhere."

"Yeah, but he's on the other side of the country. How involved can he get?"

Two days later, there's an email from Nate Dubinsky in my inbox.

Um, hope you don't mind me getting your address from Amy. I thought you might have lost mine or couldn't read my scrawl. I was just wondering how you are. Despite your stiff upper lip, I keep imagining you in a body cast. (Is that a mixed metaphor? Too many body parts?) Let me know if I did any lasting damage.

Okay, it's obvious: If you don't want to encourage someone, you don't respond. Message clear, end of story. But this isn't spam, it's Nate. The image of me in a body cast is not one I want to leave him with. So I tap out a brief message to put his conscience at rest and finish off the exchange.

I was fine, just a bit creaky the next day. So no worries and thanks for your chivalrous concern.

My inane best. I start to add how I'm glad he got home okay and hope his courses are going well, just to make sure he's yawning with boredom at the other end. But the point of my replying is to put a polite end to this communication, so I delete that last stuff. I hit send.

And get one right back. *When I came back from class today, I had a hunch your email would be waiting. Hey, I'm psychic! But don't worry, I won't be emailing you every five minutes, just wanted to say hearing from you cheered me up. I felt a bit flat when I first got here, missed everyone and everything back East, even snow. But it's been snowing a lot lately, like it's trying to make me feel at home. Here it's a big novelty. The cafeteria staff are complaining about people stealing trays and using them for toboggans.*

He was hoping he'd hear from me, he says—why? We spent a total of ten minutes alone on the way home from the party. I didn't say anything remotely witty or intelligent. He must have interpreted my lunge at him in the car as coming on to him. I guess it's possible to see it that way.

I hold off for almost a week before I weaken and reply. He writes back, just silly stuff. It doesn't feel dangerous at all. All of a sudden we have an email relationship going. I suppose he's lonely and this is how he copes. He probably has a lot of email relationships. He probably hits Send Again and replaces my address with that of the next girl on his list.

I'm the hawk, soaring, circling, waiting. Far below me, two tiny figures stand on a rock face—K-Em and me.

And then everything switches and I'm on the rock face, and K-Em and I join hands and step into space. For one brilliant moment we hang on the breeze, all promise, and then we begin to drop. The air whistles past my ears and we break through the surface, down into the cool depths. Bubbles burst and rise, floating me back up, back to the light. I burst through, taking great, sweet gulps of air. And I look down at my hands, at my body, and I'm me again. Amy! Myself.

The light is so bright I have to shut my eyes against it. I become aware of something gripping me, holding me like a vise. "I'm me!" I cry. "I'm me!"

"Mia! Mia!"

Painfully I wake up. It's Alison above me, not the sun. I'm not in the lake, I'm in bed, in my dorm.

"Mia?" Alison leans over me, her eyes big and concerned. "You were yelling. You were having a bad dream."

I struggle up on my elbow. "Oh. Sorry."

"S'okay." She turns off the light, climbs back into bed, and falls asleep at once. All is quiet, except for my thumping heart. The glowing numerals of the bedside clock say 5:01.

I've had the dream, the first time since the holidays. I go over it like I always do, trying to hold onto it. To get one more detail this time, another scrap. I can still see us so clearly, from the hawk's soaring height, our two figures on the rock. It's like when I was dying in emergency and I looked down from outside my body and saw everything that was going on. I saw myself on the bed with all those people working on me. I saw Mom and Dad outside in the corridor, hunched over on the edges of their seats.

It's at least the fifth time I've had the dream and I'm finally beginning to get that it's telling me something. I think the dream is telling me I have to go back where this all began. I've never believed in magical thinking, but hey, look at the situation I'm in, and I don't have any better ideas. I think the dream is the key.

Chapter 34

January's gone and February passes in a blur. The shop windows fill with daffodils and bunnies and pink bicycles. Along Philosophers' Walk the first white spring flowers are pushing up through the snow. Exams won't be far behind.

I'm not as scared of them as I was in the fall. I've figured out how the system works, who you talk to, how to get marks. I've learned that if I want to get group projects done, I have to be both scheduler and enforcer.

I still have to put in long hours at the books, and I do that. But I'm not as motivated as I was. I'm not thinking past the end of May. I'm leading a double life. One of them is the life I've lived for nearly three years. The other is my real one I'm going back to, the one the dream is leading me toward. I can't give much space in my head to anything besides studying, but anticipation is constantly simmering in the back of my brain.

I'm surer and surer that the dream is the key. Why else do I keep having it? For weeks I haven't been able to get the uncanny feel of it out of my head. There's that moment when I break through into the water and everything is absolutely right again.

It's not logical, I know. Why should jumping back into the same water take me back to myself? What did that Greek philosopher say: You can't step into the same river twice. But I have this sense I can't shake, that everything that's happened to me since that day in May three years ago—Ava and Avo, Loki, Susan's hair stylist Renaldo, the pay-phone episode in the bus station on that PD Day, Christmas dinner in the old folks home, K-Em and her party—all of it's simply pulled out of my head. I've made it all up. It's the longest, strangest dream, but it's a dream I'm having. All I need to figure out is how to wake up.

No amount of pinching will work. Cold water is the clue.

I've started nagging K-Em to take me to the lake. I thought I was being subtle but that didn't fool her. All along she's flat out said no. Lately, I've upped the pressure, wearing her down.

"You can trust me," I argue. "You let me come to the house and I didn't do anything terrible."

"You went downstairs. I didn't say you could do that."

"All I did was throw up. I didn't steal the family silver." And she hasn't invited me back, I notice. "Anyway, I'm not asking to go to the house again. I'm not trying to see Mom or Meaghan. I'm not asking to go to the lake when anybody else in the family is around, so you don't have to worry."

One day early in April I'm talking about how the ice must be starting to melt up in Muskoka and she whacks her hand down on the table, just missing my coffee. "Okay, okay. Quit going on about it, okay? We can go!"

"You mean that?" I'm startled.

"Yes, for God's sakes! We'll go this weekend, if that's what you want."

"No, that's too soon." I'm caught off guard. "I have to study. But, like, after my exams are done."

"When's your last one?"

"Not until the end of the month."

"Okay, well, we'll go then."

"No, we should wait until the lake warms up." This is working well. Now it seems like it's me backpedalling. "Closer to the May long weekend." I get my agenda out of my bag. I know the exact date I want. "May 19. That's a Thursday."

She checks her planner and shrugs. "Looks okay to me. I don't have anything going on then." She isn't even suspicious.

"How come you've changed your mind?" I ask.

"Because you're like a pit bull when you get set on something. And once you get what you want, like that party I had at Christmas, you move on."

Later that night she calls me. "Mom's said okay, so it's a go. I've asked Loki along too."

"You asked Loki? What for?"

"What do you mean, what for? It'll be more fun with three of us. What are you and me going to do with all that time?"

"I think it's a bad idea. Loki's not exactly the woodsman type. He'll hate it."

She goes all stubborn. "It's not negotiable. I asked him and he said yes. I'm not going to uninvite him."

I wish she'd asked me first. It's thrown a wrench into the works. I can only hope he won't be able to come after all—he has a part-time job. Reluctantly I concede. If he does come, I'll just have to work around him. "Then bring Wolfie for me," I say.

Alison is trying to get me to go in with her and a bunch of other people on our floor to rent a house at Bloor and Palmerston Avenue for next year. "I don't know about planning that far ahead," I say. If my plan works, why would I need a room?

"Mia, people have been hunting for places since January and haven't got anything this good. You have to make plans for next year. What are you going to do otherwise? Can't you afford it?"

"No, I can afford it." I go along with it, because I have to have somewhere to live in Toronto when they kick us out of res after exams. And it's a great house, actually. We'll all have rooms to ourselves, and mine is a nice sunny one on the second floor. It has a big bay window overlooking the street and comes with a decent futon and a chest of drawers. The house is sublet for June, July, and August, but we'll take over the lease in May and pay that first month's rent.

Nate writes to say he's coming back for the summer. He'll be painting houses to make some money, and he's hoping we can get together sometime. I'd like that too, but it can't happen. It's not fair to him to pull him back into this situation when I'm so close to getting out. Too bad, but I'll miss him, I say. Ava and Avo are expecting me in Kingston.

A couple of emails back Nate said he feels he can write anything to me. That made me happy, but again I wonder why he thinks that. I mean, we're almost strangers, as far as he knows. Our relationship is almost purely electronic. Against my better judgment, I've kept on with it. I only write one email to every two or three of his. It doesn't slow him down, though. I never write anything too personal. I tell him about whenever K-Em and I get together, how she's doing. I write about school stuff. I tell him I'm thinking I might switch out of commerce into development studies.

But won't you lose your scholarship? he asks.

Yes, but you have to take risks in life, I reply.

He's impressed by that. He thinks I'm gutsy.

Not that gutsy, I explain: I have a trust fund that will cover my education if I lose the scholarship. I don't say this is all fantasy anyway. If things go the way I hope, pretty soon I won't be worrying about commerce at all.

The day after our last exam, Alison and her dad and I truck all our stuff from our dorm room over to Palmerston Avenue. We can store things for the summer in a locked cupboard under the stairs. Alison's still got five times as much stuff as me. Her dad is impressed at my minimalism.

It's fun going out for Chinese food and camping out with them in the house, but after they leave early next morning for Orillia, everything feels different. The place is so big and dirty and so empty. There's nobody else here except for a weird couple who creep up the stairs to the third floor. Around eight thirty I go down to the corner and buy a coffee just to see some other human beings. The gardens all along the street are bursting with tulips and the leaves are popping. Everything is so beautiful. I decide to go for a walk.

It reminds me so much of when Nate and I were first getting together. The one time I went over to his house and we sat on the back deck listening to music, the lilacs were coming out. He'll be back in Toronto by the end of this week. I'm really tempted to stay just long enough to see him, but I know it isn't a good idea. I'd just grab him and kiss him like the last time, and things would be in even more of a mess.

After about half an hour of walking, I turn and head back towards Palmerston. My leg is starting to ache. By the time I get back to the house, I'm wiped and it's only nine thirty. I put in a call to K-Em on the new cellphone I bought to keep in touch with her. She won't be up yet, but at least she'll get my message as soon as she wakes up.

She calls back an hour later, early for her. "So what's up?"

"Nothing, really." I realize we don't ever just call to talk, just to arrange times to meet. "I'm thinking I won't stay in Toronto after all. I'm thinking I'll go back home tonight."

"But why?" She's surprised. I'm surprised myself—I didn't think I was going to say that.

"I've got nothing to do here."

"Why do you need something to do? You've been working

hard all year. You're supposed to sleep in and lie around. Watch TV. Play computer games."

That would work if I was an ordinary, whacked-out teenager, but I'm not. When I try to slow down, I speed up. I feel like some kind of droid, like there's an engine inside me trying to go into overdrive. In this lovely, steamy, languid spring world, I am an alien.

And I also know that if I've got time on my hands, next thing I know I'll be sneaking around to the house and sitting on that damn bench across the street, hoping to catch a glimpse of Mom. I pack my bags and catch the next bus to Kingston.

I wake up next morning back in my old bed feeling like I've had a narrow escape. Ava is clattering tins in the kitchen and Avo is tromping down the ramp to his greenhouse to attend to this year's tomatoes. I sit at the kitchen table in my pyjamas watching Ava take a batch of blueberry muffins out of the oven.

"Your rowing friends have been calling to ask when you are home," she says.

It's half past seven, too late to row today. But I'll be at the dock tomorrow.

Chapter 35

Two weeks later, the night before we head to the lake, I get the bus to Toronto. I'm going to stay the night at Palmerston Avenue, and K-Em will pick me up there. I'm so excited I've hardly been able to eat. Tomorrow by this time, I'll be at the lake. The day after, who knows where I'll be.

Ava loaded me up with food, including half of one of her amazing Putrid cakes. "Make sure Raymond doesn't eat it all. Make sure your friend has some too."

I kissed her and Avo goodbye, half-sick with guilt thinking I wouldn't be back. At least not back in any way that would make sense to them. And I couldn't let them see how bad that made me feel.

I said goodbye to Susan yesterday and didn't tell her my plan either. I've seen her almost every day since I came home. She hired me to set up a home office for her husband. He's going to be semi-retired by the fall, working from their house, so he needs all his files and law books where he can find them. He's nice, English, older than Susan, and just as hopeless about organizing. "Order me around," he said, so I did. It took my mind off things.

I told him and Susan I'd be gone a few days.

"You're going to Toronto? It's supposed to be hot this week-end," Susan said.

"I won't stay in the city. I'm going to a lake with friends."

"That's great, Mia." She looked so pleased for me, having friends who'd invite me for a cottage weekend. She figured I must be really coming along socially. I didn't tell her I was going back to where it all started.

It's nine thirty in the evening when I get to Palmerston Avenue. The house is dark, nobody else there, not even the spooky couple on the top floor. I let myself in, stepping over junk mail that's been shoved through the slot and left in a heap. I find the light switch, lock the door behind me, and stack the mail. I head upstairs with my bags.

The overhead light in my room is blinding, and there are no curtains. It's like I'm on a stage for everyone walking by. I hunt through the boxes I left under the stairs until I find a sheet to hang from nails left by a previous occupant. It's hardly a decorator touch, but at least it's private now.

It's creepy here on my own, so I turn on my laptop to fill the space with music. I get out my cellphone, but there are no messages. I call K-Em, but she's not answering. "I'm here," I say. "You can call me if you get this before midnight. Any time after eight tomorrow, I'll be ready."

While I wait for her to call back, I get out more sheets and make up the futon. In another box I locate my lamp, so I can turn off the overhead light. I put the chain on my door and get out the paperback I was reading on the bus.

Spiders have set up webs in every corner of the ceiling. They move busily about, checking on their catches, their shadows bobbing eerily. K-Em never calls back.

At one thirty I finish my book, a mystery I forget the minute

I turn the last page. I'm still wide awake, but I turn off the light. I don't want to be completely exhausted tomorrow. I lie in the hot darkness, listening to the unfamiliar street sounds, the small, spooky noises of the house. I think about Nate a few miles across town at his parents' house. I still remember his phone number from three years ago. We emailed this morning but I didn't tell him I'd be here.

After I come back, will he notice something's changed again? Have I let things go too far already? But wasn't the person he liked as Mia the same person he liked as Amy? Will he see that? It seems like a lot to hope.

The room is so dusty and airless I can barely breathe. My clock radio says two, then three. It's like it's never going to get light, and I'll be stuck in this hell forever. I even start wondering if I'm doing the right thing—which is crazy after all I've gone through to reach this point. I think of losing Ava and Avo and start to cry. But you'll have Mom, I console myself.

And maybe I could visit Ava and Avo when K-Em is back with them.

Finally I get up and find some paper. Suddenly I realize I need to make notes for K-Em about what I've been doing for the past couple of years. I've already told her about Susan, told her that Susan knows, even if she doesn't like it. "Tell her we've switched back, and she'll help you," I write.

I tell her she doesn't need to go on with the commerce program. People knew by the end I wasn't happy. Still, I think as far as exams went, I probably got As and Bs. She'll have those to put toward a degree. "Think about switching to another program," I tell her. "Or just do whatever you want."

"Be good to Ava and Avo. Talk to Ava about cooking. Talk to Avo about tomatoes."

It's not going to be easy for her, picking up life where I left off. It's not going to be easy for me either, picking up hers. I try to imagine going to one of her modelling jobs. What on earth do models do? Actually, forget modelling. I'm not doing that.

Before anything happens, K-Em and I can come back here to Palmerston Avenue. She can go to Kingston on her own, or Loki can go with her. How is he going to handle it? It might be a step too far, even for him.

And I'll get into the Jeep and drive home with Wolfie. Let myself in with my/K-Em's key. I'll walk into the kitchen, open the fridge, and pour myself a glass of skim milk. "Hi, Mom!" I'll shout, if she's in the house. "I'm home. I really missed you!"

At 4 a.m. it's still pitch dark, but the birds start to sing in the trees. And then I guess I fall sleep for a little while, because I have the dream. The sky is a quivering blue bowl. The hawk is circling overhead. This time I know I'm dreaming, and I know what I have to do. I take K-Em's arm and step out into space. I fall straight down, back to myself.

By eight I'm packed and ready. K-Em calls at nine, her voice groggy like she just got out of bed.

"Have I got time to run out and pick up some groceries?" I ask.

"If you want to. We were going to get some on the way."

She and Loki turn up at eleven. By then I'm in a seriously unhinged state. Loki jumps out of the passenger's seat and takes my bags. Wolfie is in the back seat navigating, eyes on the road, keen to get moving. I start to slide in beside him.

Loki stops me. "You take the front. I got my tunes. You guys can talk."

K-Em looks like she's modelling leisurewear in a striped T-shirt and denim mini, her shiny black ponytail sticking out the back of her cap. "I thought you might have changed your mind," I mutter as I buckle in.

"About what?"

"About going to the lake."

She rolls her eyes like I'm out of line. "We're just running a bit late."

I try to relax as she turns onto Bloor, then up Bathurst to the 401. Loki's bopping away in the back, plugged into his iPod. It's a beautiful, sunny day, perfect for heading to the country, if only I'd had more than an hour's sleep. I adjust the air conditioning and my seat. "Did you bring a bathing suit?" I ask K-Em.

"I've got plenty up there. But it'll probably be still too cold to swim."

She seems in a good mood. I'm in a seriously bad one, which I didn't expect. I thought I'd be euphoric. I know I'm just tired and anxious. So much depends on what happens next, and so much could go wrong. And also I don't like her driving. She's changing lanes jerkily, speeding up and slowing down, driving me nuts. I'm afraid she's going to kill us.

"Want me to take over?" I ask as she veers onto the exit to Barrie. The guy behind us lays on the horn and swerves around us. I haven't driven since the accident, but I know I could handle the road better than her.

She raises an eyebrow. "You got a licence?"

"Yeah, the one you're driving on."

"I earned it," she says proudly. "I took lessons. Everybody figured it was brain damage because I didn't know how to drive, but I'd never driven. I mean, I wasn't even sixteen. And where was I going to get my hands on a car, living in care—other than stealing one?"

Her driving settles down a bit so I don't push taking over. "The weather report says it's going to be really hot tomorrow," I say. "The lake probably won't be warm enough, like you say, but there's another place we can swim." I mention it offhand, like I've just thought of it.

"The quarry."

"Yeah, it's a great place. Have you been there?"

"I *know* about the quarry, Mia."

"What do you mean, you know?"

"I mean, I know all about the quarry. That's where it happened. You won't get me anywhere near there. Forget it."

She's looking straight ahead, so I can't see her expression. I'm not risking an argument at this point. I turn up the radio and we don't talk much until we get to the lake.

When we're about twenty miles away, Wolfie starts panting. Once we're off the highway I open my window so he can stick his head out. I get dog slobber on my shoulder, but I don't mind. We pass the turnoff to the quarry road. I almost point it out but change my mind.

Wolfie bounds out into the marina parking lot as soon as the door is half-open, and leads the way to the dock. It takes ages to load up the launch. K-Em and Loki have brought a ton of stuff—food, beer, sleeping bags, DVDs. K-Em oversees everything. "The weight has to be distributed evenly so we don't tip."

Excuse me, but I know that. It's majorly pissing me off that she knows how to do the things I used to. "Wolfie, get in the stern," I tell him. "Good boy." He and I sit together. I dip my hand into the water to test it—still pretty cold. It will be warmer at the quarry.

K-Em has trouble getting the engine started. The boat is an old mahogany launch my dad restored. I lean between her and Loki and push in the choke half an inch. "You flooded it. You'll have to wait five minutes and try again."

She frowns and waits thirty seconds. It starts.

Loki's still wearing his ball cap and shades and listening to his music. He's in a boat on a beautiful lake in the great outdoors, but he could be anywhere. I tug one of the buds out of his ears as we roar off. "You're not in Kingston now," I shout.

He glares but he puts his music away.

"You want to take the wheel?" K-Em asks him. He shakes his

head, but she insists. "Come on, try it!" She scrambles over him on the seat. Now he's steering and she's bouncing and squealing whenever we hit a little wave. He's actually laughing. I don't think I've ever seen his teeth before.

When we get closer to the island, I start worrying he'll drive us up on a shoal, but they shift places again and she steers us safely in around the rocks. We round the point, and there it all is—the dock and the boathouse, the sloping red granite shore, the dark pines above. My old rope swing still dangles over the water. It's so dear and familiar my head swims.

As we approach, I point up to the window above the boathouse. "That's where I'm sleeping." It's my old room, my private clubhouse.

"Fine with me," says K-Em. "It's probably full of bats."

We stagger up the path with as much as we can carry. K-Em unlocks the door. "Let me go first, okay?" I say. She steps aside and I walk in. The smell brings tears to my eyes.

Loki is right behind. He sniffs the air loudly. "Something died in here or what?"

"It'll be okay once we open all the windows." K-Em turns on the propane to run the stove and the fridge. Mom has had the place painted again. The woodwork is dazzling white and the pine floors are gleaming.

Once Loki opens beers for us all, he goes prowling in and out of the rooms. "Hey, rich girl!" he shouts. "This place has gotta be worth millions, right?"

She catches my eye, embarrassed.

He points to the paintings on the wall. "That some of that Group of Seven shit?" he asks.

"If it was, what would it be doing here where anyone could break in and steal it?" I point out.

We go out to sit on the screen porch where it's breezy. A heron flaps past just as Loki is stretching out on the couch. He shoots up from the cushions and retreats inside the cottage. "What the hell was that?" he yelps. "It looked like something out of *The Lost Planet*!"

"I can't believe you haven't seen herons before," I say. "There's always one standing on the rocks by the rowing-club dock."

"I didn't know they could fly," he says.

Chapter 36

By now it's nearly six o'clock and we're all ravenous. I bought a barbecued chicken and a loaf of Portuguese bread this morning. K-Em dumps a package of baby greens in a bowl.

After we've eaten and cleared the table, Loki gets out a stack of at least a dozen DVDs. There's enough to keep us going for days, which is not what I came for. Wolfie and I head to the boathouse.

My old room up above the water is dark and about a hundred degrees. I unhook the shutters to let in light and air. I don't think anybody's cleaned the place since I left. I get the broom from behind the door and sweep out the debris and the cobwebs. By the time that's done, I'm streaming with sweat.

In the boathouse below the old red canvas skiff is still on the rack. It's an antique, probably a hundred years old. It looks dusty and neglected, like nobody's used it in years. Maybe I was the last person to take it out. I clean it with the broom as best I can. It's a struggle lugging it to the water. I should ask Loki to help but I'm too impatient.

Wolfie is barking and leaping around. He loves going out in the boat—too bad he can't help carry it. The canvas rasps the concrete as I lower it to the water. I curse myself and hope I haven't scratched the paint. I manage to take some skin off my shins.

Finally the boat is in the water, gently tugging on its rope alongside the dock. Wolfie leaps in the stern and sits expectantly.

"Just hang on a minute, dude. We need oars." I get them down from the rafters and find a life jacket and safety pack. A minute later I'm pushing us out onto the lake.

The oars aren't right for my short arms and the seat is grimy. Wolfie is soaking wet from a quick plunge, and water from his coat collects in muddy rivulets in the bottom of the boat. Dad would be yelling his head off at the mess. But Wolfie grins at me, tongue lolling. It doesn't take much to make him happy, the big goof.

I lean into the oars to find my rhythm. The water rushes along the hull. The lake has the golden calm of early evening, and I'm skimming over it like a water bug. As I skirt the island, I check off from memory every boulder, every aspen and birch along the shore.

At the nearest point to the next island, the one that belongs to the Duffys, I strike out across the channel. No signs of life at the Duffys' cottage, but for sure some of the family will be here this weekend. The summer I was thirteen, I had the worst crush on Jim Duffy, an older guy of seventeen. I must have rowed past their dock a dozen times a day, hoping to catch a glimpse of him, waving casually when I did. When all the kids were swimming together, he used to splash me, which I took as a sign that he liked me. Then he broke my heart by inviting his city girlfriend up for a visit.

I imagine Jim stepping out onto the cottage deck and seeing me now. Would he think, *Is that Amy out in the skiff? Funny, it doesn't look like her.*

A loon calls from the far end of the lake. It's so idyllic I'm lulled into thinking everything's going to be okay. But then my anxiety rushes in again, and I turn back. Tomorrow's getting closer by the minute and I don't have a strategy in place. I manage to get the skiff out of the water without doing much more damage. It'll be safe enough on the dock. Later I'll get Loki to help me put it away.

In the cottage Loki and K-Em are well into the first movie. Loki is way beyond his mother's chick flicks now, but I don't know if it's that an improvement. Everything he's brought looks depressing— he even has the horrible Bergman one about a medieval plague. Right now they're watching something lighter, an old Hitchcock classic called *The Birds*.

"How'd they get all those crows to stand still like that?" I ask. There must be thousands of them.

"They're not real, they're models," Loki says. "Cool, eh?"

"Come and watch with us," K-Em says, but getting creeped out is the last thing I need. My mind is racing about tomorrow and how I'm going to set it up. How I'm going to get some time alone to talk to K-Em. I wander around the cottage distracting myself, finding stuff from my childhood, old kids' books. I read out some choice passages from a Sweet Valley High novel. "Can't you just be quiet?" K-Em says. "We're trying to watch some culture here."

"Since when is pecking eyes out culture?"

"When it's Hitchcock," Loki says. He gets up to get another beer from the cooler. "You better have another."

"I'm sick of beer." I rummage in the sideboard where the booze is kept, and lo and behold, find a half-full bottle of gin. I haven't had a gin and tonic since Dad made me one, which was years ago. Of course nobody thought to bring lemons, but I open a bottle of Sprite.

K-Em and Loki are sprawled on the couch, ankles coyly entwined. I keep saying how stupid the film is, Tippi Hedren driving an outboard in a silver mink coat. I finish my gin and tonic and make myself another big one.

I'm in the kitchen when K-Em's cellphone rings in her bag on the back of the door. She doesn't even hear it over the screaming seagulls in the movie. On the third ring I pick up.

"Amy?"

It's Mom.

"No." My voice comes out croaky. "It's Mia. Amy's friend."

"Oh, Mia!" She sounds really pleased. "I've heard so much about you! When are we finally going to meet you? Amy keeps promising to invite you around."

I swallow. "That would be nice." *I'm having a conversation with Mom.*

"It's so great that the three of you could get up to the lake. You know how much she loves it there. No break-ins or mice infestations, I hope?"

"No. Everything's fine."

"You'll all be very careful, won't you?"

Suddenly K-Em is beside me, hands on her hips. "Who are you talking to?"

"We'll be careful," I say into the phone. "Here's Amy now."

Loki pauses the DVD and goes outside for a pee. I take the place he's vacated on the couch while K-Em talks to Mom. She doesn't talk very long. A minute later she stalks back and sits on the far end of the couch from me.

"I didn't say anything to her I shouldn't," I protest. "Just hello and stuff. Then I passed it to you."

"Because I heard you talking." She looks over at me. "But all right. Whatever. Are you okay?"

"Yeah." Just kind of shaky. Weird to be talking to Mom after so long. And I'm so tired, running on empty for sleep. I take a deep breath. "I know you don't want to go to the quarry, but I really need to go back and see it again."

K-Em stares at the paused image on the screen, blood-covered children, their mouths open, running from the birds. "Why? I don't want to go. I told you, I've never wanted to go there."

"Aren't you even curious? I mean, it's where this all started."

"Not for me. I can count, Mia. I know why you want to go. Tomorrow's May 20—the date it happened. Three years ago tomorrow. I'm not stupid, even though you think I am."

"I never said you were stupid."

"I never said *said*. I said *think*. What do you want to do—jump onto the rocks and nearly die again? I was in traction too, remember? You want to go through that all over again? Are you nuts?"

"Well, we're not going to go down to Yonge Street and walk in front of a truck."

"You're right about that." Her mouth is a thin line. "This has been your big scheme all along, hasn't it? You want to jump on those rocks again, and presto! We'll be right back to our old selves. I'm right, aren't I? Aren't I? How dumb is that?"

"Nobody's going to land on any rocks," I protest. "I'm not crazy. I just want to jump. I just want to feel the water close over my head and come up and get on with my life. Then I can put it behind me. I know it doesn't make sense, but humour me, okay? Is that so much to ask?"

She folds her arms and makes a snorting noise. "If you want to go so badly, then okay, go. Why do I have to get dragged along?"

Because of the dream. The dream's very clear—we both have to be there. But I can't tell her that.

The screen door bangs. Loki is looking from one of us to the other, alarmed. "What was all the yelling about?"

"We were not yelling," K-Em says. "She wants to go to the quarry where the accident happened. I'm just telling her I'm not going."

He takes her side, of course. "It's a stupid idea, Mia. Forget it."

"Forget it!" Now I really am yelling. "How can I forget it? I'll never, ever forget it."

Wolfie gets startled by the noise and starts barking. I leap up from the couch to storm off, and several things happen at once. I knock over my glass, and it shatters on the floor. My weak leg buckles, and as I stagger, trying to get my balance, I step on the glass. I feel it pierce my foot and I scream. Wolfie barks even louder.

"Oh, God, look at the blood!" K-Em steps around me. "What the hell did you do that for? Now we'll have to take you to the hospital."

"I didn't do it on purpose!"

"I know, because you're drunk!"

Loki makes me sit down while K-Em gets a flashlight lantern and shines it on my foot. She leans in closer and suddenly I feel a sharp, searing pain. I shriek.

She holds up a bloody shard of glass. "I got it out. It's not really cut, more a puncture."

"I'll have to get a tetanus shot."

"Maybe not. The glass was clean. Nobody used it but you."

"It was on the floor in all the dust! What about mice droppings? I'll probably get infected with hantavirus."

"The gin would have killed the germs."

She doesn't care if I get tetanus. After all, I'm the only thing that stands in her way. She's taken my body, my family, my life. The only thing that's spoiling it is me wanting it back.

She gets a basin of hot water and some rubbing alcohol, cleans my foot and dries it with paper towels. "Cool your jets. It's stopped bleeding already." She tapes some gauze around it.

She does a pretty good job, and I start feeling less upset and paranoid. I don't really want to go to the hospital. It's in Minden, which is hours away.

"How do you know first aid?" I mumble.

"I used to do it on my mother all the time. She was always getting polluted and bashing or cutting herself."

She doesn't mean Mom—she means Krystal's mother. That sets me off again. "You admit what's happened to us, *Krystal*. You know what I've been through. You have to come to the quarry with me. You owe me that much."

"Crap. I don't owe you anything."

"What about my life? What about my mother?"

Her voice goes hard. "Okay, I feel guilty, all right? I got a better deal than you did. But things were rotten for me before, and I'm not going to give it up again, okay? Why should I?"

Loki shoves a mug of water and some pills at me. "Calm down, Mia. You better take these."

"What's for?"

"It's just Tylenol. For the pain."

"Why do I need Tylenol for a cut foot?"

"Come on, take it."

He seems awfully interested in getting those pills down me. Suddenly this voice in my head says clear as anything: *Those pills aren't Tylenol. He wants to drug you. They've brought you here to kill you.*

I push Loki out of the way and flee out the door and down the path to the boathouse. Slamming and locking the bottom door behind me, I scramble up the stairs and lock that door too. I shove a chair under the doorknob, the way they do in movies.

I'm panting and my heart is going like a piston. A minute later I hear knocking below. "Mia, let me in." It's her.

"Leave me alone," I yell back. "I'm tired. I'm going to go to sleep."

I hear the two of them out there talking in low voices. The knocking goes on. Loki shouts, "Come on, Mia, open up!"

"You can have Wolfie for the night," K-Em wheedles. "He'll make you feel better." Very cunning, but I'm not falling for that.

I take the chair away from the door and shove the iron bed frame against it instead. I'll spend the night on the floor on the mattress. If they break down the door, I'll slash the screen and dive into the lake. I'll swim to Duffys' island and if they try to come after me, they won't be able to see me in the dark.

After a while I don't hear voices anymore. The only sound I hear is the water lapping below me in the boathouse. Maybe they've given up and gone back to watch their movie. Or maybe they're just pretending. My head is pretty sure they've gone, but my body's still terrified. The tiniest noise—rustling leaves, a twig snapping—

freaks it out all over again.

Everything's a mess. I'll never get her to the quarry after this.

But I have to. The dream says it's my only hope. In my bones I know that's what the dream is telling me: *It's the only way*.

I have a desperate idea. There used to be a gun in the cottage. Dad kept one in the sideboard drawer for emergencies. I could wait until they're asleep and creep in and get it. The keys to the Jeep are in K-Em's bag on the back of the kitchen door. Between the gun and the keys, somehow I'll get us to the quarry.

But even I can tell I'm not thinking straight. I've never used a gun and I'd be terrified to fire it. There's two of them and one of me, and I don't think Loki would just sit there while I took K-Em away at gunpoint. This is not the way it's supposed to happen. None of this is anything like the dream.

Chapter 37

I start up in terror at the sound of hammering. *They've come back!*

It takes a moment to figure out the noise is coming from inside my head. I open one eye and shut it quickly against the bright glare: daylight. I struggle to free myself from something wound tightly around my ankles.

Slowly the room comes into focus. I'm still in the boathouse, still in my clothes, tangled in the quilt. The awful pain is a hangover.

But the pounding continues. "Mia, you okay up there? Come on, open the door."

I drag the bed frame aside and unlock the top door. There's a twinge of pain from my foot and I look down in surprise at the bandage around it. How did that get there? Then I remember. Gingerly I make my way down the stairs, trying not to jar my brain. Unhooking the bottom door, I open it a crack.

K-Em is standing there in a tank top and red running shorts, Wolfie behind her. "What was going on with you last night?" she demands. "Are you okay now?" She holds out a steaming mug of coffee. My head swims with the smell.

"I thought you might need this. You take milk, right?" When I open the door an inch wider, she pushes the coffee into my hand, then takes a bottle of water from the waistband of her shorts. "And this too. I'm going for a run. Drink the coffee if you want it, but get that water inside you. We're going to the quarry later."

What? "Did you say *quarry*? You'll go with me?"

"I'll go," she says grimly, "if it means that much to you. But I don't like the idea. You'll owe me big time. Go back to bed and sleep it off. You look like shit. And drink the water."

Then she's gone. I stand blinking after her. The sunlight still hurts my eyes. The birds are making a horrible racket. Slowly I make my way back upstairs, spilling coffee as I go. I drag the bed to its regular place, heave the mattress and sheets on it, and lie down.

My watch is still on my wrist. Nine o'clock, it says. Outside the screen window the lake glitters in the sun. The reflection plays across the rafters.

I check the seal on the water bottle. It's intact. *Paranoia will destroy ya.* My terror of last night is fading, but it's not entirely gone. Why are we going to the quarry—so they can push me off?

I lean back against the wall and contemplate the mug of coffee gently steaming on the windowsill. I reach for it and hold it under my nose. I can't resist. I sip.

Then I hunt around until I find my bag. I dig out the email from Nate I printed out just before I left Kingston.

Why are you always writing to me about Amy? I want to know about you. Not one more word about Amy. I want to know about Mia.

I feel like we've known each other for a long time, even though you tell me I hardly know you at all.

When I wake up next, it's nearly eleven. I move my head cautiously. It's still sore but I feel better. The coffee couldn't have been poisoned. And, amazingly, we're going to the quarry.

I unwind the gauze from my foot and check the cut. It's not even that tender to the touch. I find some Bandaids in the top drawer of the dresser and put one on in place of the gauze. Then I change into my bathing suit, go down the stairs, out onto the dock, and dive.

Yow!

I make myself take ten strokes before I turn back and scramble up the ladder as fast as I can. Drastic action, but it works. My head is much clearer. I don't know what their plan is, but it's going to get K-Em and me to the quarry. From there I'll have to play it by ear.

Once I've towelled myself dry and warmed up in the sun, I change into a T-shirt and shorts—who cares if my scars show?—and go up to the cottage for breakfast. Or maybe lunch.

I don't see K-Em, but Loki is reading a film magazine at the porch table, his hood up.

"Sorry about last night," I say. "You know me and booze."

"You missed the rest of *The Birds*. It was fantastic. Weird ending."

"It was that woman wearing the mink coat," I say. "She was an invasive species. The birds had to drive her off."

He flips the magazine page. "Hey, makes sense."

"Where's K-Em?"

"Getting changed. I'm not coming. I'm staying here and keeping Wolfie company. She doesn't want him at the quarry. He might try to jump in after you guys."

"You don't mind?" I try to make a joke of it. "You don't want to dive into a whole bunch of pond life?"

He doesn't smile. "I still say it's a bad idea. I don't like it. If she wants to go, it's her business, but if anything happens to her—"

The threat hangs in the air. "What? You'll what, Loki?"

He meets my eye. "I won't forgive you, ever," he growls. "Just be careful."

"I plan to. Don't worry." He should worry, though.

K-Em comes in carrying a beach towel. She's wearing a

bathing suit under her shorts. "I'm ready. Let's get this over with."

Loki and Wolfie come down to the dock with us. K-Em doesn't hug them or anything, just jumps into the boat. What's going through her mind?

I untie us and hop in after her. As we roar away, I look back and see Loki and Wolfie still watching us. *Goodbye.* When we come back, everything will be different.

Chapter 38

It's beautiful out on the water. People are already arriving for the long weekend. They pass us going in the other direction and wave. We wave back, like we're out for a spin, like we're going to pick up extra ice at the marina.

Once we get to the dock and the Jeep, I navigate us to the quarry. It's only a couple of miles, ten minutes away at most. K-Em complains about the ruts and potholes. "What kind of a crappy road is this?" she mutters. Usually she's not so irritable.

"Let me drive," I offer.

"Never mind." She revs the engine through a sandy spot. "How much further is it?"

"Just after the bend."

But when we round the corner, I see something that makes my heart stop. There's a makeshift rail fence across the road all snarled with barbed wire. And a hand-painted sign in big angry red letters: NO DIVING. PRIVATE PROPERTY.

K-Em stops the Jeep and leans back in her seat. "I guess that's the end of the road. Well, we tried."

I fling open the door and run across and start tugging on the wire. She turns off the engine and comes over. "What are you doing, Mia! You'll cut yourself!"

"Somebody's made a hole already. We can break through and walk the rest of the way."

"You'll rip yourself to shreds!"

"They can't keep us out. Give me a hand!"

She just stands there. "Maybe we shouldn't be doing this after all, Mia." Like the barbed wire is some kind of sign.

But finally I bend the wire enough to make a big enough hole to slip through. K-Em goes back to the Jeep and gets our towels and other stuff, a life jacket. I hold the top wire so she can duck under. The quarry is only fifty yards or so further.

Between my hangover and the strain, I feel like I'm in the Hitchcock movie from last night. There isn't a bird to be seen or heard, but the whole scene is weirdly Technicolor, banks of lilacs blooming on a lunar landscape of rock. We come out of the bush, and suddenly we're looking down into clear water.

The quarry at last.

I lead her up the sloping path, pushing though the scrub, then stop on a jutting ledge. "Right here. It was exactly here." Below, glimmering under the surface are the rocks I landed on. I pull my T-shirt over my head.

"It's awfully high," K-Em says in a small voice. Her hair is damp with sweat at the nape of her neck. "I didn't think it would be so high. Isn't there a lower ledge where we can go in?"

"It has to be this one." She can't back out now. "You promised."

"I didn't promise!" She takes a step away from the cliff face. "I didn't promise anything. I didn't even say I'd go in the water. I came along to make sure *you* didn't kill yourself."

It's now or never. "Please, K-Em." I blurt it all out. "I keep having this dream that we jump and go back to the way we were. I've had it over and over. It says we both have to jump. I believe it. I believe that's what it's saying. None of this is real, K-Em, don't you see? We're dreaming it. This is the only way we can wake up."

"You're crazy. I don't want to." Her jaw is tense, her face ghostly white. It's naked fear I'm reading on it. Any stupid thoughts I had before about her having some plot to get me out of the way are gone. There's just her and me. I don't know why she said she'd come, but she's here.

"You have to jump too. You don't have to dive. In the dream we jump. Do it for me. Please." I'm begging.

"How high do you think it is?"

"Twenty-five feet or so. Not that high. You couldn't really hurt yourself unless you belly-flopped."

"You're out of your mind, Mia. *You* hurt yourself."

"Only because of the rocks. We can see them better today. We'll jump well away from them, over there where it's deeper. It'll be safe. I promise."

"I don't like deep water." She picks up the life jacket she's brought.

I take it from her. "That's not a good idea. It'll cut into your arms when you hit. You can swim, can't you?"

"Not very well."

"Two strokes and you'll be back to shore. I'll be right beside you. I'll make sure you don't drown."

She shakes her head. A pulse is beating in the top of my skull. What can I say? What can I do to convince her? I hold the life jacket out over the edge and let it go. We watch it tumble down and land on the surface. "There. It'll be waiting for you."

She gives a kind of whimper. Finally she begins to pull off her tank top. We strip to our suits in silence. I'm too terrified to talk anymore. I look up, and there's the hawk, soaring, flying on the wind! I point up. "See that hawk, K-Em? It's in the dream. It's a good omen. Are you okay?"

She nods unhappily. "Okay." Her voice is so small I can barely hear her.

I reach for her hand and squeeze it. We're both crying.

Goodbye, Ava, goodbye Avo. Goodbye, Nate.

"Thank you," I say. "Thank you, thank you, Krystiana. No matter what happens, I'll owe you forever."

Her eyes are wide with terror. I fix mine on the hawk. As I leap out from the rock, I feel her pull back.

But at the last second she jumps, she's with me. We fall together. It's like slow motion, like in the dream. Time stands still, like my whole life is about to unfold in front of my eyes.

And then my toes touch water and I'm through. The quarry closes over my head in a hard rush of bubbles. The shock of impact forces our hands apart. I lose her.

Down, down.

At last I stop myself from sinking any further. I kick back up to the light. Then I'm back in the air, gasping.

I look around for K-Em. I can't see her. I'm all alone. The life jacket bobs on the surface, but she's nowhere near it. Where is she? Where has she gone?

I duck my head under the surface again. The rocks loom in the green stillness a few yards away. The bottom drops off steeply. No sign of her. Not even any bubbles.

The cut sides of the quarry are like canyon walls. I dive and push myself down into the shadows and along until my lungs are burning. And again. I promised Loki I'd make sure nothing happened to her. I promised her!

I see it all unfolding all over again—rushing for help, ambulances, divers. Mom crying. I kick back up to the surface and gulp air. I shouldn't have done it. I shouldn't have made her do it.

"Mia!"

And there she is, crouching on the rocks behind me.

I fling myself over to her. "I couldn't see you!" we both scream at once.

Her long black hair is plastered to her pale shoulders. Nothing has changed.

I scrabble up on the rock beside her and clutch her. She puts her arms around me, long, strong arms. "It's okay, it's okay." She holds me tightly and pats my back as I sob.

"It didn't work."

"No," she says softly.

"But you did it for me. You did it for me."

"Because I just knew it wouldn't work. You're so smart, Mia, but you didn't know it wouldn't work."

"Why didn't it work?" Then I remember: It wasn't the right day! It happened on a Friday. "It should have been a Friday! We'll have to wait until it's the right day and date. It'll work then!"

"No, Mia." She shakes her head. "We'd have to die first. It won't ever work."

We climb back up to where we left our towels. The hawk is nowhere in sight now. I'm still crying as we crawl back through the barbed wire. I don't duck low enough and the wire scores a deep red line down my shoulder. In the Jeep, K-Em blots it carefully with the end of her towel.

She takes my face in her hands. "Is it really so bad? We're both grown up. We'd probably have left home by now anyway. If you want to see Mom, you can, okay? As long as you don't tell her. And you can see Nate. He was there at the hospital, he'll understand. Loki understands—Nate will too."

"No, he won't."

"Give him a chance. At least try."

When we get back to the cottage, I head for the boathouse. She grabs my arm. "Don't do anything stupid. Promise?"

I just nod. I climb the stairs, strip off my wet suit and let it fall to the floor, crawl into the rumpled bed. Almost at once I'm asleep. I don't dream the dream. Outside the window, gulls fly past. Next time I rouse myself, swallows are skimming the water. Then it's bats against a crimson sky. How long have I been sleeping? Hours.

I push off the covers and set my feet shakily on the floor. The boards feels rough and warm. Is it really so bad, like she asked me? If it had worked, like in the dream, everything would have been another mess. K-Em would be stuck trying to go on with university. And poor Loki, what would he do? I don't think even Loki could cope with another switch.

I feel around the side of the bed until my fingers close on Nate's email. I hold it against my face, against my eyes. *Why are you always writing about Amy? I want to know about you. I want to know about Mia.*

Maybe he'll get that chance. I don't know if it's fair to him or not. Maybe I have to let him decide. Then I think, he's got two more years out West, maybe more. A lot can happen in that time. Eventually, maybe, people can get used to anything.

And I decide, like Scarlett O'Hara in the old *Gone with the Wind* movie Mom always loved, that I'll think about all of this later. I have time.

Acknowledgements

This story, like most I have written, started out a long time ago, when I was about twelve. It set up a terrifying fantasy: Cut off from my home and family by some terrible, unimaginable event, what would I do to get them back? It was an ambitious project, and I soon got discouraged and bored with it. Also, I was missing a major piece: if I, the narrator, was miraculously transported into someone else's body, what happened to the body's original owner?

I picked up the idea again after many years, mostly because I needed new work to bring to my weekly writers' group. The Ban Righ Tuesday Writers' Group sat through every word and responded with their usual gentle candour, helping me iron out some stubborn narrative knots. I'm very grateful to Kris Andrychuk, Bill Hutchison, Christina Decarie, Darryl Berger, Tanya Ambrose, Danielle Gugler, Robert Clark, and Nancy Brown. Special thanks are due to Nancy, who put in extra time urging me to go deeper.

Thanks to Linda Pruessen, my publisher and editor at Key Porter, for her sure-handed guidance, and to Marie Campbell, my agent at Transatlantic, for her support. And thanks, as always, to George Lovell, enthusiastic and loyal supporter, who listened to the whole manuscript not once but twice between Kingston and Vermont, and to my brother Robbie for his comments. I lean heavily, as ever, on my daughter, Leila Garvie, whose meticulous reading saved me from many embarrassments.